M000158123

THE BOOK OF THE DEAD

THE BOOK OF
THE DEAD

Elizabeth Daly

FELONY & MAYHEM PRESS • NEW YORK

All the characters and events portrayed in this work are fictitious.

THE BOOK OF THE DEAD

A Felony & Mayhem mystery

PRINTING HISTORY
First edition (Farrar & Rinehart): 1944
Felony & Mayhem edition: 2010

Copyright © 1944 by Elizabeth Daly
Copyright renewed 1971 by Frances Daly Harris, Virginia Taylor, Eleanor
Boylan, Elizabeth T. Daly, and Wilfrid Augustin Daly Jr.

All rights reserved

ISBN: 978-1-934609-56-9

Manufactured in the United States of America

Library of Congress Cataloging-in-Publication Data

Daly, Elizabeth, b. 1878.
  The book of the dead / Elizabeth Daly. -- Felony & Mayhem ed.
     p. cm.
  Originally published: New York : Farrar & Rinehart, 1944.
  ISBN 978-1-934609-56-9
  1. Gamadge, Henry (Fictitious character)--Fiction. 2. Book collectors--
Fiction. 3. New York (N.Y.)--Fiction. I. Title.
  PS3507.A4674B66 2010
  813'.52--dc22
                              2010004885

CONTENTS

The icon above says you're holding a copy of a book in the Felony & Mayhem "Vintage" category. These books were originally published prior to about 1965, and feature the kind of twisty, ingenious puzzles beloved by fans of Agatha Christie and John Dickson Carr. If you enjoy this book, you may well like other "Vintage" titles from Felony & Mayhem Press.

———◆———

For more about these books, and other Felony & Mayhem titles, or to place an order, please visit our website at:

www.FelonyAndMayhem.com

or contact us at:

Felony and Mayhem Press
156 Waverly Place
New York, NY 10014

Other "Vintage" titles from

FELONY&MAYHEM

THE BOOK OF THE DEAD

CHAPTER ONE

Nobody

THE SICK MAN SAT UP IN BED motionless, watching the doorway and listening. He could hear nothing but the low murmur of his all-but-silent electric fan, an occasional sound of traffic in the street far below. Traffic was dead; it was midsummer in 1943, the fourth day of the heat wave, and pleasure driving was banned.

He was carefully tended. The agreeable, melancholy face against the glassy-smooth pillows was closely shaven, the light hair brushed until it gleamed. His long, fine hands lay flat on a linen sheet of the finest quality, which had been drawn up and folded back across his knees. His thin blue pajamas might have been fresh from the laundry. The table beside his double bed held books and magazines, a jug of ice-water, a writing block and a fountain pen. There were awnings in the four windows; the large, high corner room seemed cool and pleasant.

He raised his left wrist to look at his watch; the leather band slipped along his arm. Noon. The doctor not due for an hour, Pike busy in the kitchen with the early lunch tray: he glanced across the room at the telephone, which stood on its stand just within the doorway.

After a moment of indecision he threw back the sheet and swung his legs off the bed. He stood upright, steadying himself against the table, and then walked slowly towards the telephone. When he reached it he stopped again, listening. A big living room separated him from the lobby and the kitchen beyond, but sounds now came to him—the clink of glass and china. He sat down in front of the telephone and took the directory from its shelf below.

Balancing it on his knees, he searched his memory; then he opened the book and turned pages, at last running his finger down a column. He paused at a name, memorized the number, and replaced the book on the shelf. As he put out his hand to the telephone the doorbell rang clearly.

He withdrew his hand, got up, and was half way to a window when a tall, redfaced, thin man in a white jacket looked in at the door.

The man said: "Having a little exercise?"

"Yes. Cooling off."

"That must be the doctor; he's early." The man spoke in a casual kind of drawl. "Better go back to bed."

The sick man was looking a little frightened. He smiled, however, as he answered: "Will he think it matters?"

"So long as he doesn't think I'm neglecting you." The other now had him by the arm, and assisted him competently back into bed.

"He won't think that, Pike." There was a sardonic note in the patient's voice.

"I won't tell on you, anyhow." Pike pulled the sheet up, smoothed it, arranged a pillow, and then went at a leisurely pace out through the living room.

He came back with a big and rather fat elderly man, dark and untidy, whose lowered head and vast forehead made him look rather like a buffalo. He carried a black bag.

"Well, Mr. Crenshaw." The doctor came around the bed, put the bag down on the floor beside him, and laid his fingers for a moment on the sick man's wrist; but it was only a ritualistic gesture, and he took the fingers away.

"Well, Dr. Billig."

The doctor sat down and looked around him. Pike, leaning with his hands on the footboard, stood nonchalant; his long face was not the face of a servant, the white serving-coat did not match its weatherbeaten look; his easy slouch of a walk was not a servant's toddle. He was as immaculately clean as his patient, but his brown hair was ragged; his light eyes had a humorous look, and as he watched the doctor he smiled.

Dr. Billig, glancing at him, did not return the smile. He said: "Nice and cool you are in here, anyhow; it's a terrible day, Mr. Crenshaw. My patients didn't show up, so I cut office hours to drop in on you."

"You look pretty hot yourself, Doctor."

"You don't, Mr. Crenshaw."

Crenshaw smiled. "I know how lucky I am."

Billig looked at him and looked away. Beside the white bed and the groomed sick man he was not only shabby and unkempt; he was grubby. And he was not at his ease. His big pale face lowered, his yellow-brown eyes in their yellowish whites roved and shifted. He said: "But you'll be better off in hospital now, Mr. Crenshaw."

"Bad as that?" Crenshaw's pleasant expression did not change. An attractive face, the doctor thought; but if there ever had been strength in it, illness had washed all that away.

"Just so you'll be more comfortable. Trained service. You certainly get good care from your man here—" Billig's eyes went to Pike's face and left it. He took out a crumpled silk handkerchief and patted his damp forehead. "But I'd rather you had nursing from now on. You'll be in clover at St.

Damian's. I've got you a corner room, what do you think of that? And you'll look out on big trees. I must say I like those oldfashioned places myself."

"It certainly wouldn't be considerate of me to die here," said Crenshaw. "When do I go?"

"This afternoon, if you like."

"If I like? When you've made all the arrangements, and the hospitals are all jammed? Of course I'll go. But don't send me in an ambulance. I'm like Disraeli," said Crenshaw. "I don't like the emblems of mortality."

"Certainly you can go in a cab. I'll come along myself and see you settled there." Billig put his handkerchief away. He looked relieved. "Glad to see you there."

"You've been good about it, Doctor; letting me alone, I mean. I suppose they'll bother the life out of me at this hospital?"

"Nothing of the sort."

"It beats me why they won't leave a man in peace. I know the prognosis—"

"Because you insisted on knowing it."

"—they know the prognosis. Why all the fuss with blood transfusions and X-rays when a man's dying?"

"We agreed that you weren't going to let your mind dwell on it, Mr. Crenshaw."

"No; but I must arrange my affairs, such as they are. Pike, I'll have to get to the telephone; I'll want the bank to send a man up with my balance. I'm paying my way in cash." He glanced at Billig. "You know what happens when a man dies; no checks cashed, nothing paid until the estate gets ready to pay the bills. None of that for me. I shall pay your bill in cash, Doctor, and I shall deposit a couple of thousand at the hospital for my expenses there and for my burial expenses. I suppose the hospital will take care of that for me?"

Billig frowned. "Of course, if you like."

"There's nobody to do it for me, you know. But will that couple of thousand be enough? That's what you must tell me, Doctor. Shall I be at St. Damian's more than a week or so?"

Billig said shortly: "Absolutely no telling, Mr. Crenshaw."

"If you would only realize that I don't mind talking about it. Do I, Pike?"

Pike said: "Mr. Crenshaw don't mind at all."

"I simply want to leave enough cash. I'm to be sent up to the old family plot in Stonehill, Vermont, you know; where I've been settling up my uncle's estate." He laughed. "One old frame house, and money in the bank to bury *him*. The smart old boy had an annuity. I haven't one, but there's a copy of my will at the bank here; the original is in my bank in California." He turned his head on the pillow. "If there's a residue at the hospital, let them apply it to their charities."

Billig looked at Pike, and continued to look at him until that personage took his hands from the bed rail and walked out of the room. The doctor waited until he had presumably got out of earshot; then he said in a low voice: "Mr. Crenshaw."

"Yes?" Crenshaw did not turn his head.

"I wish there was somebody we could notify."

"I told you there wasn't."

"Nobody?"

"Nobody."

"Not out there in California?"

"Business acquaintances."

"Not in Vermont?"

Crenshaw paused a moment. Then he said: "I was only in Vermont about my uncle's estate; I was greatly surprised when I heard that he'd left me the old house. I told you, Doctor; our branch of the family settled in California, they're all dead. I haven't a soul belonging to me but some cousins in or near Omaha, if they're still on earth—I don't know. I haven't seen any of them since I was a boy there in the summers. They're not in my will," he added, laughing, "and I don't think they'd bother to come east for my funeral! I assure you that I wouldn't go to Omaha for theirs."

Billig sat silent, his big hands on his knees. After a minute he said: "It's rather a responsibility."

"Why?" Crenshaw turned his head to look at him.

"If you've forgotten somebody, and the person asked why nobody was notified—"

"I haven't forgotten anybody. I like to be alone, Doctor." Crenshaw looked past the other, into a vastness of space and time. "I don't mind dying alone. I think people have a right to die as they choose—if they can. You've left me in peace, Doctor, and I'm very grateful. I won't alter my will; it was made many years ago, and changing it would be too much of a bother for me now. But I'm paying you two thousand dollars in cash; a thousand today, before we go to the hospital, and Pike will hand you another thousand in cash after I'm dead."

Billig, his face pale and blank, sat back in his chair. His short-fingered hands were clasped and his thumbs rotated slowly. After a long silence he said: "I have no right to two thousand dollars, Mr. Crenshaw."

"Right? No. It's not a question of right; it's a question of my regard. You diagnosed the case and told me the truth about it when I asked for it; you've taken every care of me for two weeks, you've made arrangements at the hospital, you'll see that my wishes are carried out. What I pay you is my business, and nobody else's."

Billig cleared his throat. "Except this Pike's."

Crenshaw laughed. "Don't worry about Pike; I have every confidence in Pike. Perhaps you don't know the type?"

"You picked him up in Vermont."

"Well, not off the street! I'll tell you exactly what happened. I came east by request of my uncle's bank in Unionboro, Vermont. I was sole executor. I'd never laid eyes on the old gentleman, but I suppose he had some sentiment about the last scion of the elder branch of the family. I stopped in New York on May twenty-eighth and took this apartment for the summer; thought I'd stop here on my way back to San Francisco—I hadn't been east in years. It was a sublet, nicely furnished; I saw the advertisement in the paper. I was looking forward to seeing the sights—if there were any to see.

"I travelled around a little, and reached Unionboro on—let's see—the fifteenth of June. I found that Stonehill is five miles out, up the mountain. This man Pike was at the station with his old car, and as there was a shortage of taxis—of course—I let him haul me and my bag. We talked, and he amused me. He's a character, typical Yankee failure and drifter, perfectly satisfied with himself; had been peddling some gadget or other until the factories didn't deliver and he was out of a job.

"My uncle's house is a couple of miles north of Stonehill; and I found that thanks to him I could stay there instead of at the so-called hotel in Stonehill. He's a regular jack-of-all-trades, cooked for me like a chef. Pretty soon I began to feel pretty weak and sick, and he did everything; got provisions, supplied me with newspapers, everything. He made me comfortable. I'm glad I had that interlude, Doctor; it was a pleasant, quiet time, and it's beautiful up there in the mountains. And I got a pretty good idea of Pike's character. He's as honest as the day."

Billig, looking at the sick man from under heavy lids, said nothing.

"Then I crashed—on July the third, as you know. Pike sent word here that we were coming, got me down by the afternoon of the sixth, and then ran out and found you; first sign down the street. He's done everything for me. Now his job's over—here. Tonight he'll go up to Stonehill to close the old house and pay all outstanding bills and settle things. When the funeral's arranged for he'll get your second thousand to you."

Billig said gruffly: "I'm obliged to you."

"The obligation is mine. I don't know," said Crenshaw, smiling a little, "what Pike will do now. I'd be willing almost to swear that whatever he does he won't settle down. It's too late for him to change his ways; he's in the forties, like me. I couldn't change *my* ways to save me."

Billig looked quickly at his patient, but the profile on the snowy pillow did not change; Crenshaw was not aware of any special meaning in his phrase. He went dreamily on: "He may have come down in the world, or perhaps," he laughed, "subsided. But you can't always tell about these New Englanders; I don't know where they get the manner from, but the plainest of them often have it—very cool and grand."

"Have you anybody up there to check on him, Mr. Crenshaw?"

"Everybody in town will check on him. They all know him. The real estate agent will keep an eye on the house, too, before and after Pike leaves it, because it's going into the market. Pike won't run off with Uncle's Franklin stoves. The house won't sell, of course; it will fall to pieces. Run-down farm and orchard, pump and no drains."

"Well, you know your own business best." The doctor stooped sideways, picked up his unopened bag and got to his feet. But he still lingered a moment. At last he said in a monotone: "Neither of us is a sentimental man; but let me say that when my turn comes, I hope I'll behave as well as you're doing."

"Behave?" Crenshaw turned his head to look at the other, and then put out his hand to a little radio that stood on the lower shelf of the bedside table. He turned the dial. "Let me tell you something, Doctor," he said, and waited until the record of a string orchestra began to play. He listened, turned the music lower, and then lay back. "There's one thing," he said, smiling, "that I've been good at all my life; bowing to fate.

Lying down on my face, if necessary. Well, here I am on my back. It might be worse."

"It might indeed. I'll be around for you when the day cools off—if it ever does. Say five o'clock?"

"We'll be ready. Will they let me have those nice tablets of yours if I'm restless at night?"

"You'll get them."

"Sedatives always make me feel like a rag in the morning, but I prefer that to a long night."

"You'll have your phenobarbital."

Billig lumbered out of the room, through the living-room and into the lobby. He came face to face with Pike, who was bringing a tray from the kitchen. It was set out with a delicate luncheon, at which the doctor glanced as Pike set it down on a side table and opened the door.

Billig asked, without looking at the manservant: "Has he really nobody?"

"Far as I can make out, not a soul. How long has he got, Doc?"

Billig did not raise his eyes to the inscrutable lean face above him. He said: "Perhaps two weeks. Can't say," and went out into the hall.

Pike closed the door after him, and picked up the tray. He carried it into the bedroom and set it down. While he cleared the bedside table, Crenshaw, watching him, spoke:

"It's our last day."

"I haven't much packing to do. I've been getting things together." Pike's careless drawl did not change. He added: "But I can't find that book."

There was a silence. Then Crenshaw said: "Stupid of me. I must have left it on the train."

"Unless you want it, why worry about it? I could go out and get you another."

"I have a feeling that I shan't be doing much reading from

now on. Don't give me my lunch yet, Pike; call the bank. They can't send a man up with the money at a moment's notice."

"That's so."

"And I must have the check ready for him. Where's that checkbook?"

"On the desk."

"What's the balance?"

Pike opened the checkbook. He read: "Four thousand five hundred and sixty-seven."

"That ought to be enough, even if I stick it out longer than Billig thought. From what he said at first, it oughtn't to be much more than two weeks."

"Don't worry." Pike went across to the telephone, got the book, found a number, and dialled. He asked: "This the Western Merchants Bank of New York?" and after a moment: "Hold the wire, please. Mr. Howard Crenshaw will come to the telephone."

CHAPTER TWO

Somebody

ON WEDNESDAY, July the twenty-eighth, the heat closed down again; it was as hot as it had been on the same day the week before. But it never seemed really hot in Gamadge's library, which ran the whole width of the house in the rear, and had a through draft across the hall to the windows in front. Gamadge had an early dinner that night, so that his old colored servant Theodore could go to the movies. He sat afterwards beside one of the long library windows, drinking his coffee and smoking a cigarette.

He was alone, except for Theodore and the big yellow cat Martin. Clara was on Long Island; she had gone protesting, but Gamadge—choosing to consider her in a delicate state of health—had insisted on her renting a friend's cottage beyond Southampton. She had entrained in late June, accompanied by her chow Sun, the cook Athalie, and the maid Maggie. Gamadge was supposed to spend his week ends with her, but two appointments would keep him in town this week until Saturday.

The city was curiously still; as still, he thought, as it must have been long before he was born, when his grandfather sat in this same window after dinner smoking a cigar and drinking coffee from this same blue cup, or another of the set. His grandmother would have been taking the country air south-west of Albany, within sight of the Catskills. They would have been surprised at the changes in the house, the house to which they had come after their honeymoon; outside it was much the same, a modest three story and basement brick dwelling with a low stoop and white trim; but indoors it now combined business and living. The basement was given over to Theodore and Athalie; the drawing-room was Gamadge's office, the dining-room his laboratory, the pantry his dark-room. A little elevator—just big enough for two—had been installed behind the stairs; a dumb waiter rose from kitchen to library, where the Gamadges had their meals.

The laboratory apparatus was shrouded in dust-cloths now; Harold, Gamadge's assistant, was off somewhere in the Marines, and Gamadge's work was all war work, conducted with a certain discretion in a cubbyhole of an office that over-looked Bowling Green.

He now sat looking out at the big ailanthus tree in the back yard, his feet up on a chair and the radio going. But he heard the elevator stop in the hall; Theodore came to the door.

"Somebody to see you, Mist' Gamadge."

This form of announcement meant that in Theodore's opinion, the caller was respectable, but of not quite enough importance to have a sex. Gamadge said: "Describe."

"Young person, or anyway not over thirty. No card. No name. Says it's business. She's from the country, or was."

"Selling something?"

"I don't think so. I'd say a school teacher, but she ain't used to telling people."

"Office worker?"

"Kind of oldfashioned for that, Mist' Gamadge. I don't place her."

"Why should I see her without an appointment?"

"She wouldn't come unless she had a good reason."

"Oh; wouldn't she? I'll take your word for it." Gamadge removed his feet from the chair, shook himself together, and went downstairs. Before going into the office he opened the front door a little and put it on its chain; then he entered the long room with its molded ceiling, and faced his visitor.

She had been sitting on the edge of one of the deep leather chairs; when he came in she rose, and stood firmly planted; a middle sized young woman, with a round, rosy face, round brown eyes, and wispy brown hair. The hair was covered by a turban, evidently home made, of brown ribbon; it was decorated with a pink rose. She wore a brown linen suit, and brown Oxford shoes that had seen wear. She clasped a large brown woollen handbag.

Gamadge thought: She's naturally self-possessed, but shy of this call. He said: "Good evening."

"Mr. Gamadge?"

"That's me."

"My name's Fisher; Idelia Fisher."

"Sit down, Miss Fisher, while I get a little air for us." He went to the closed window, which was fitted with an air filter. He turned this on, made a face at the resulting flow of warm air, unlocked and raised the window. Then he turned a chair to face her and sat down himself. "What can I do for you?"

"I don't know if you can do anything." Her voice came through her nose, but it was too forthright to be disagreeable. She went on: "I know I ought to have telephoned and asked for an appointment."

"Well, it's safer; I mightn't have been at home."

"I know; but there might have been a secretary. I know how they are—I'm one myself." She gave him a dry smile. "I couldn't have said what I wanted to see you about. It's bad enough to tell *you*!"

"Bad enough?" He returned the smile.

"You might think I was crazy."

"I promise I won't."

"I wouldn't have even thought of coming and taking up your time, only for what Mr. Macloud said last summer."

"Mr. Macloud?"

"He said he knew you."

"If it's Bob Macloud, the lawyer, he certainly does."

"He has this summer place up near where my aunt lives in Vermont. That's where my family comes from—Stonehill, Vermont. I live in New York now, because I work here; I'm my uncle's assistant—he's a dentist. I go back to Stonehill summers to stay with my aunt, and Mr. Macloud drives over for cakes and turkeys."

"But not this summer."

"No, he wouldn't come because he couldn't use his car. But last year he came, and there was something in the papers about you—and your wife."

"There was," agreed Gamadge, grimly.

"Mr. Macloud told us about you." She was gazing at him shyly, with a kind of puzzled speculation.

"Well," said Gamadge, laughing, "Macloud's a lawyer. What he told you isn't likely to have been defamatory."

"He said that when queer things happen you sometimes…" She paused, and was silent for so long that Gamadge at last prompted her:

"Yes, Miss Fisher?"

"Mr. Gamadge…" She brought it out desperately: "I haven't any money."

"Oh. You mean for a fee?"

"Yes."

"Don't worry about that. Tell me the queer thing. As Bob told you, I like them."

"I don't know how I had the nerve to come. I haven't told my aunt or uncle; they live in Hartsdale. They'd think I was crazy. You don't know anything about me," said Miss Fisher, more coherently than a pedantic listener might have been willing to admit.

Gamadge was not pedantic. "Any friend of Macloud's is a friend of mine," he said, "and I don't repeat professional confidences to anybody. Has this peculiar thing happened here in New York?" He thought fleetingly of an oldfashioned dentist's parlor, in which the dentist's niece officiated without uniform, make-up, or intimidating technique. His own dentist's receptionist was decorated like an Ouled Nail.

"No," said Miss Fisher. "Or at least it didn't start here. It started up in Stonehill this summer; on the twenty-first of June. At least it was outside of Stonehill, up in the old Crenshaw house. That's where I met Mr. Crenshaw. But he came down to New York on the sixth of July, and now he's in hospital, and nobody will tell me a thing."

Gamadge waited.

"Mr. Gamadge," she went on, "I never realized before. Anything could happen to a person in this town, and nobody like me could ever find out a thing—not a single thing."

"Well, that depends; I think you exaggerate. However, I don't know the story."

"It just came over me after I called at the hospital last night. A person like me can't get into places, nobody answers questions, and I never felt so helpless in my whole life."

"I couldn't get information about a patient in a hospital, Miss Fisher; they don't give it out. You have to get hold of the doctor, or a relative or friend."

"He *hasn't* anybody!"

"This Mr. Crenshaw hasn't?"

"That's what he told me. Nobody."

"Except you." Gamadge smiled at her, but she went on with her round eyes fixed earnestly on him:

"I'm not anybody. That's the trouble. They wouldn't tell me anything at the apartment, or last week at the hospital, or last night."

"Did you come to me hoping that *I'd* get information about Mr. Crenshaw for you?"

"I just—just want you to tell me what you think."

"I'll tell you what I think." Gamadge took his cigarette case out of his pocket and offered it to Miss Fisher; he had expected her to refuse a cigarette, and she did so—by shaking her head.

"May I smoke?" he asked.

She was surprised at the question. "Why, yes."

Gamadge lighted his cigarette. He was thinking: "She's not in love with this man Crenshaw. She may be romantic, but she's not the kind that loses her head. She's not flighty, she's not a fool."

"I'll just explain the whole thing from the start," said Miss Fisher. "I get a long vacation every summer, when my uncle and aunt go to the shore. I go up to my Aunt Julia's in Stonehill, because I couldn't afford to go anywhere else; I only have to pay board."

These family arrangements, thought Gamadge, how greatly they depend on the Aunt Julias.

"It's nice up there," continued Miss Fisher. 'But there isn't much to do—Stonehill is just a village, up in the mountains five miles north of Unionboro; about all I do is take walks. The best walk is up beyond the old Crenshaw farm, two miles out. Old Mr. Crenshaw lived there until last spring, when he died. I used to go around back of his house and come out above, and follow the road on to where it ends; there's a nice view. This summer I thought I could sit in his orchard; since he was dead and the house closed, you know.

"On the twenty-first of June I started out on that walk, and before I got to the house I turned off up a field to a stone wall, thinking I'd climb over it and sit in the orchard. When I got over the wall, I nearly died; there was somebody sitting on the other side of it, sitting up against it, with his hat over his eyes. It was this Mr. Howard Crenshaw. He was just as nice as he could be; he said please go right ahead through the property, or sit there if I wanted to; but excuse him for not getting up, he hadn't been feeling well. We got talking."

Gamadge said: "I don't like to interrupt; what did or does he look like, your Mr. Crenshaw? I always like to know."

"Well, he's about forty-five, I should say; he has very light hair and blue eyes, and he has a nice quiet way of talking. He had nice clothes, and a Panama hat. He was rather pale, but I think his skin is that way naturally—he doesn't sunburn or tan. He was medium sized, rather thin. Clean shaven."

"Very good sketch."

"Just nice-looking. He told me about his uncle leaving him the old place, and about his coming all the way from California to see about it and settle the estate. He said he'd met a man-Pike—in Unionboro, and this man was very good at cooking and so on, and they were kind of camping at the house. I don't wonder; the hotel isn't any good any more."

"What was Pike like?"

Miss Fisher said in a different voice: "I didn't see much of *him*. He was some man with a Ford car who drove Mr. Crenshaw up from Unionboro when he got there from New York; on the fifteenth of June, that was. When I met him they'd been at the house nearly a week. Mr. Crenshaw just took a fancy to Pike; said he was a philosopher. Anyway, they were settled in the house, and Mr. Crenshaw said he hadn't had such a nice vacation in years. He'd never been in Stonehill before. He intended to stay till sometime in July, and then go back to New York for awhile.

"Well, we ended that first time by climbing up to the top of the orchard, where you can see over the valley and across the mountains; and you can see the road to Stonehill for half a mile, until it goes around a bend.

"Mr. Crenshaw told me that Pike had been selling something on commission, and had lost the job on account of shortages, and that he didn't know but that he'd take this Pike back to New York with him; he wasn't well, and this Pike just suited him.

"While we were talking, Pike came around the bend in the road and along in his car; he'd been getting groceries in Stonehill. Mr. Crenshaw got up rather fast, and said: 'There's Pike now. I won't keep you.'

"Well, of course," and Miss Fisher gave Gamadge her dry smile, "when people say they won't keep you, they mean they don't want to be kept."

"So they do."

"I had a feeling that Mr. Crenshaw didn't want Pike to see me. I didn't mind. I know how these country people talk, and I didn't want to embarrass Mr. Crenshaw. I just went off through the woods south of the orchard, and hit the road further down. I came back the next day, same time, but a little earlier. Mr. Crenshaw asked me to."

"It isn't often that we have the luck to meet congenial people by the wayside."

"I never met anybody like Mr. Crenshaw! I don't know why he ever wanted to talk to me. But we had the nicest talks, and he said he looked forward to them. He'd read everything, and he was so interesting. I didn't realize that he must have been getting sicker all the time. He never said so."

"What was the trouble?"

"He didn't say."

"And you never met Pike at all?"

"I saw him on the road a couple of times, and once in Stonehill. Mr. Gamadge…Mr. Crenshaw was afraid of him."

"Crenshaw was afraid of his tame philosopher?"

"It wasn't just on account of the gossip; I knew that the first time, but I didn't realize it till I thought it over, going home. When Pike's car came around the bend Mr. Crenshaw was frightened."

Gamadge considered her thoughtfully. "You were convinced by Crenshaw's expression?"

"I was convinced that he was afraid to have Pike see anybody on the place, talking to him. When he hustled me off that first time I was embarrassed, and I just thought—you know; that Mr. Crenshaw was afraid of its getting around in the village—our meeting in the orchard. Then, on the way home, I realized that there was more to it than that."

"You didn't read more into Mr. Crenshaw's expression than was actually there? Perhaps you didn't like to think that he was afraid of gossip."

"Mr. Crenshaw didn't let me come on Sunday, when Pike didn't go down to the village for groceries and newspapers."

"Oh. I see."

"Mr. Crenshaw said he rested on Sundays. Why should he? He rested all the time. But that wasn't all, either, Mr. Gamadge." She looked down at the bulging handbag on her lap, opened it, and exclaimed in annoyance when several small objects fell out and dispersed themselves on the floor.

Gamadge begged her to sit still while he retrieved them. He restored her door key to her, a leather stamp-case, a collection of dress-samples fastened together by a pin, and a cardboard rectangle upon which Gamadge commented as he handed it over:

"You don't smoke, Miss Fisher; why carry paper matches in your handbag?"

She looked amused. "It fools everybody."

"Fools everybody?"

She opened it, and held it out for his inspection. "Well, I'll be hanged." He peered at it. "A nice little sewing kit."

"Darning kit," said Miss Fisher with satisfaction. "It's cute, isn't it? I got it at a department store, at the notion counter. It has four little reels of imitation silk, and two needles, and I carry it back and forth to the office. I don't live near the office now, I moved over to the west side on Monday. It's a rooming house, and of course there's only the telephone in the hall. That's one reason why I wanted to get in touch with Mr. Crenshaw, if I could; to tell him my new address. Nobody knows it yet except my aunt and uncle in Hartsdale. And I wanted to return his book."

She put her hand into the bag, and with some difficulty extracted a brown octavo, somewhat the worse for wear.

"Mr. Crenshaw lent me this," she said. "It's a Shakespeare, one of a set. He brought it with him to read; he said he always liked to have some Shakespeare to read when he went on a trip. He forgot it when he left; I wouldn't like him not to have it—it has his grandfather's name stamped on it."

She showed Gamadge the name in gold—*Elisha M. Crenshaw*—on the cover.

"Family book," said Gamadge, looking at it with some interest. "How did he come to forget it, I wonder?"

"Because he left in such a hurry; I came up on the sixth of July, and the house was shut up, and they were gone."

"Really."

"Mr. Crenshaw lent me the book because we'd been talking about things—the war, and so on, and he wanted me to say whether I thought human nature changed much."

"A broad question."

"He was awfully interesting; he liked to talk about such things. He wanted me to read *The Merchant of Venice*—about Shylock, you know, and how he felt, and the way they treated him. He wanted me to say whether I thought Shakespeare meant him to be a comic character."

"If he meant that, all I can say is that he had a funny way of expressing it."

"I didn't get a chance to read it. But I saw the marked passages in another play, and after that I was afraid of Pike seeing me."

Gamadge raised an eyebrow.

"You may think I'm crazy," continued Miss Fisher in an apologetic tone. "Perhaps I am. I'd seen Pike on the road once before. After I read those marked passages I saw him twice again, not very close; he was in his car. He was just an ordinary country feller, only he looked kind of pleased with himself; but I was glad he never had seen me up there talking to Mr. Crenshaw, and I was glad he didn't know I knew Mr. Crenshaw, or who I was."

"That's interesting." Gamadge's eyes were on the Crenshaw Shakespeare. "What did he look like?"

"He's around forty, thin, rugged looking, sunburned—the way farmers are; with rough-looking brown hair and a sharp nose, and these sharp, light eyes. He always wore shirtsleeves and an old felt hat, and needed a shave."

"What was terrifying about him?"

"Nothing, except that Mr. Crenshaw was afraid of him—"

"Afraid he'd see you," amended Gamadge.

"Afraid of him," repeated Miss Fisher firmly, "and marked the passages in the book. I never had a chance to speak about them to Mr. Crenshaw; the next time I went up—on the sixth of July—they were gone. I made sure they were gone, and then I climbed in."

"Climbed in?"

"Through a back window; those catches aren't much, and the house wasn't boarded. I was bound and determined to find out where Mr. Crenshaw had gone to—if I could." She added, with some dignity: "I didn't care to ask at the post office. Mr. Crenshaw hadn't told anybody he knew me, and I wasn't going to tell anybody I knew him."

"Very proper."

"I looked at all the thrown-out papers I could find, and in the bottom of a coal-scuttle I found this."

She offered Gamadge a newspaper cutting which looked as though it had been carried about in a wallet. A marked item read:

> *Sublet. May 1st, October 1st. Large living-room, dining-room, bedroom. Kitchen, maid's room, two baths. Telephone. Unusual. Apply on premises.*

There followed an address on upper Park Avenue.

"I thought," said Miss Fisher, "that Mr. Crenshaw had this in his wallet when he engaged the apartment in New York, the one he told me he'd taken for the summer. I also found an envelope in the bottom of the coal-scuttle, with the address on it; but it had been addressed wrong and corrected, and thrown away. What I think is that the coal-scuttle was full of papers, and they were thrown on the fire in the stove, and these stuck. They were covered with dirt and dust, and nobody noticed them. I threw the envelope away."

"Upon my word, Idelia," said Gamadge, admiration making him forget formality, "you don't seem to need much help in getting your man; but it wasn't like you to throw the envelope away."

"I didn't see any reason to keep it, since I had the address on the clipping."

"You hadn't had difficulty in finding Crenshaw then; but you can see that it constitutes better proof that he went to the apartment than the clipping does."

"I couldn't get in touch with him at the apartment at all. I didn't like to write; after all, he did forget all about me and the book; but I thought he ought to have his book, and I thought I'd wait till I came down to New York myself, and then telephone. I came down on the fifteenth, and I telephoned; they said he was there, but that he had a private wire, and they couldn't ring him."

"A telephone is advertised in the clipping. It means that there is no switchboard in that apartment house, or that that particular apartment has no telephone connection with the house system."

"So they said. They wouldn't give me the name in the book."

"Wouldn't they?"

"No, the man said they weren't to give out telephone numbers. That's when I began to feel so helpless."

"They had you, I must admit; being a sublet, the apartment telephone wouldn't be listed under Crenshaw's name; not unless he notified the telephone company."

"He hadn't. I tried them."

"He doesn't seem to have craved communication by telephone with the outer world."

"He hadn't anybody; and I did begin to feel as if he was cut off."

"Not by Pike, though; he had his freedom at Stonehill. He could have walked away from the place while Pike was in the village."

"Just the same, I didn't send the book; I was afraid Pike might get hold of it. Mr. Crenshaw didn't want him to know he knew me—"

"Knew anybody, didn't you decide?"

"Knew anybody, then: and there were those marked passages—and words rubbed out in the margin."

"Words rubbed out?"

"You can't read them; but they were there. Anyway, I didn't send the book. But I thought I'd go up to the apartment some night, and see whether I couldn't leave it with somebody, and pay him to give it straight to Mr. Crenshaw. I hated to go. Finally, last Wednesday after office hours I telephoned again—

to find out if he was still there. They told me he'd just gone to St. Damian's hospital. They didn't know why, or for how long, or they wouldn't say."

"Well, he must be safe enough at St. Damian's hospital—wherever that is; I never heard of it."

"It isn't far from the apartment; a big old place with a wall around it, in its own grounds. I went over there that night and last night, and they said he was resting quietly."

"That's what they always say."

"Last week I left my name and address; I thought it would be all right to do it now—Pike wouldn't be at the hospital. But tonight there was no message."

"We haven't a leg to stand on, Idelia; I could pull wires and try to get information for you about Crenshaw's illness, but for reasons that occur to me vaguely I might not succeed in getting it. You didn't send his book up to him; why didn't you?"

"The girl in the office there was so uninterested, I thought it might not get to him at all until after it had been in the hands of strangers. He may be very sick," said Idelia in a low voice. "He may have been very sick when he left Stonehill. I thought before we did anything about the hospital that you might look at those marked passages and those rubbed-out words. Perhaps you could bring them back again. Mr. Macloud said you could do anything with handwriting—anything at all."

CHAPTER THREE

The Crenshaw Shakespeare

GAMADGE TOOK THE VOLUME of Shakespeare from Idelia, turned it in his hands, opened it, closed it again. "Macloud's compliment was never deserved by me," he said, "and is deserved at present less than it ever was. I haven't done any work in the laboratory—or any to speak of—since my assistant came to me five years ago. I was the fellow that sat back and told him what I wanted done there. Now he's away off somewhere, and I'm not in the document business at all any more. But I like the feel of Mr. Crenshaw's book. I like the look of it."

"Those marked passages—" began Idelia.

"Let's look at the book first, inside and out; advance from the general to the particular, inquiring as we go. I'm dying to see the marked passages," admitted Gamadge with a smile, "but I didn't even take the book in my hands until I had your story. Now that I am actually holding it, I see that it's Volume I of a set of six. It's an octavo, thickish, bound in polished brown calf and nicely tooled and gilt. Who did you say was Elisha M. Crenshaw?"

"Mr. Crenshaw's grandfather."

"It's a family book, a nice possession, but its binding is in a deplorable condition, and its title-page informs me that it is not an edition hotly desired by collectors. Its market value is nil.

"The binding is rubbed, so rubbed that it deposits reddish-brown smudges on my trouser-leg; that's old calf for you! The back is falling off; half of it, in fact, *has* fallen off," remarked Gamadge, catching the broken piece and laying it on the corner of his desk. "But the book itself is solid, and when we open it we find that except for a good deal of foxing—I mean these brownish spots—the fine, tough paper is in mint condition, the pages like new.

"Mr. Crenshaw's grandfather's firm but faded signature runs across the top of the title-page—a bad habit of our ancestors. Below we find:

THE PLAYS OF WILLIAM SHAKESPEARE
In Six Volumes
Vol. 1.

And below that again is a little engraving in outline of the three witches, whiskered and bearded, and resembling three indignant old gentlemen in night attire. They're pointing to a battle."

"There are lots of pictures," said Idelia.

"So we find from the description on the next page:

Harper's Fine Edition—Numerous Steel Engravings.
The Dramatic Works of
William Shakespeare

Time, which is continually washing away the dissolute fabric of other poets, passes without injury by the adamant of Shakespeare.—Dr. Johnson's preface.

Harper & Brothers, Cliff-Street
1839

"And it *is* a nice edition, but clear and bright as the type is, it's close and it's rather fine. It would try your eyes, Idelia, to read Shakespeare in this edition, unless by the brightest daylight.

"Turning the page, we arrive at *Life and Writings*, by N. Rowe, Esq. Then we have Dr. Johnson's preface to the edition of 1773, hereinbefore quoted. Then we have an *Essay on the Learning of Shakespeare* by Farmer. Hum. *The ever-memorable Hales of Eton* (who, notwithstanding his epithet, is, I fear, almost forgotten)...Ho hum. Then we get Observations on *The Tempest*, and then at last we get *The Tempest* itself. Odd."

"Odd?" repeated Idelia.

"Odd arrangement of the plays. The first play in the first volume was Shakespeare's last. The second is *Two Gentlemen of Verona*, an early play; then *Merry Wives of Windsor*, a jolly play; then *Measure for Measure*, a gloomy play; then *Comedy of Errors*, a funny play; and last *The Merchant of Venice*, which has about everything in it, including a spot of tragedy. I don't know what the editors had in mind when they got up this edition; perhaps it follows the pattern of an earlier one; but what we want to know is, Idelia, why did Mr. Howard Crenshaw bring this volume along with him on his trip east?"

Idelia looked blank. "Why shouldn't he?"

"Well, he couldn't possibly have wanted *Two Gentlemen* or the *Comedy of Errors* for desert island reading; or, unless he's a Falstaff fan, *The Merry Wives of Windsor*. People usually choose a volume of the great tragedies or the coruscating histories for such a purpose. However, we have left *Measure for Measure*, *The Merchant* and *The Tempest*." Gamadge's greenish eyes regarded Idelia reflectively. "Have you read The *Tempest* lately?"

"I don't know that I ever have read it."

"There's a play for a desert island! There's a play for an invalid! A calm, philosophical, resigned, after-glowish kind of play. In certain circumstances—circumstances of ill-health, deep trouble, abiding sorrow, you couldn't go wrong with *The Tempest*." Gamadge opened the volume and glanced casually at a page. He read: "...*after which, to a strange, hollow, and confused noise, they heavily vanish.* What a play. I wonder how they produced the noise; don't you, Idelia?"

Idelia asked: "Who vanish?"

"Nymphs and reapers."

"Reapers?"

"Only visions, you know; part of Prospero's little games. Pretty soon he gives them a brush-off: *avoid;—no more.* And then he goes on from there into the sublime...Was Mr. Howard Crenshaw fond of *The Tempest*?"

"Both the marked passages and the rubbed-out pencil marks are in *The Tempest*."

"Ah! What did I say? He brought the book east for the sake of *The Tempest*. In other words, Mr. Howard Crenshaw was feeling middle-aged and—not quite well. He was escaping."

Idelia looked startled. "He didn't talk about that play."

"No indeed. He didn't talk about his illness."

Idelia was silent. After a pause she said: "The marked passages are right at the beginning of the play."

"And here's the first one: Act I., Scene I. Dear me."

Idelia looked triumphant.

Gamadge slowly read the marked passage aloud:

I have great comfort from this fellow: methinks, he hath no drowning mark upon him; his complexion is perfect gallows. Stand fast, good fate, to his hanging! make the rope of his destiny our cable, for our own doth little advantage! If he be not born to be hang'd...

"Well!" exclaimed Gamadge. "Your friend Mr. Crenshaw didn't like somebody, that's evident. You think the somebody was his handyman, don't you?"

"Perhaps we'd know if we could read what he wrote in the margin."

Gamadge lifted the book to peer closely at the faint indications of pencilled writing opposite the marked words in the text. "Gone, all gone," he said. "He rubbed and he rubbed, but he didn't rub out the ghostly message that something was there. Let's see the second passage...Here it is, Act II., Scene II. Three passages, to be exact:

...this is a very shallow monster:—
...a very weak monster:—
...a most poor credulous monster:—Well drawn, Monster, in good sooth...

"And what are we to make of these? If the first one referred to Pike, these certainly don't. Can they possibly be a biting attempt at self-criticism? Is Mr. Crenshaw referring to himself?"

"I thought they might mean that he was in Pike's power."

"You don't need an investigator, Idelia; you only need a leg man. Here's the second marginal comment, or rather its traces, all down the page. He wrote very lightly and with a hard pencil; he rubbed hard. I may not be able to reconstruct these notes."

"But you'll try?"

"Well, he didn't mean anybody to read them, Idelia." Gamadge looked at her in some amusement. "He probably rubbed them out before he lent you the book so that you shouldn't read them. Ought we to drag them back into the light of day from no higher motive than intellectual curiosity?"

"I'm not curious. I only want to be sure that he's all right."

"I'm curious, curious as anything; but we must try to dig something out at the hospital before I have a go at this job. I don't much look forward to it. I wonder—I very much wonder—whether he'll thank you for all the trouble you're taking in his behalf."

"He'll never know. I won't tell him."

"But when he gets well again, and you resume your pleasant friendship, you and he may laugh together over the whole episode; including your unauthorized entry into his house above Stonehill, Vermont."

"I don't believe it's a thing he'll ever laugh about. Mr. Gamadge—how could you bring those pencil marks back again?"

"Or read the traces of them? Well—there are several ways. There are the cold fumes of iodine; they condense on the paper and bring out all sorts of things. But the trouble is that the paper has to be photographed immediately, or the recreated marks die away. As a one man job it's not the handiest in the world; and it had better be a one man job—we don't want accomplices. If we did, I should send the book to a friend of mine who would get it treated in a police laboratory."

Idelia looked frightened.

"Then there's what they call the addition method," continued Gamadge, "but let's not go into that; it's very complicated; you use collodion plates and I don't remember what all. Then there's the diapositive method; and there's polarized light with crossed Nicols. You don't want to know about crossed Nicols, do you?"

Idelia shook her head.

"I'm glad you don't. My assistant Harold would have been delighted to instruct you, but I've never used them myself. Then there's the dodge by which you photograph the back of the paper in an oblique light; that may bring out traces of the writing, and that, God helping me, I shall try if I must."

Idelia sat despondent. "It's terrible. I ought to have known that it would be. Mr. Gamadge—if Mr. Crenshaw is in trouble, and we get him out of it, he might be glad to pay you."

"Those underlined passages, let me repeat, don't sound as though he would thank us for getting him out of trouble. Don't worry about my getting paid. Hang it all, I have the apparatus; I ought to lick this if Harold could. And I'm getting interested—" he opened the Shakespeare again, and smilingly turned pages—"deeply interested in the problem; for it is one. Will you leave Mr. Crenshaw's book with me for the present?"

"You'll have to have it if you work on those rubbed-out marks."

Gamadge rose, went over to one of the steel filing cabinets, and locked the Shakespeare away. He came back to his guest, but remained standing beside her. "Shall we go up to St. Damian's?" he asked.

Idelia got out of her chair as if worked by a spring. "Now?"

"It's only a quarter past eight; why not? Hospitals admit visitors in the evening until at least nine o'clock."

They went out into the hall. Gamadge picked up his hat from the console that had probably held three-cornered hats in its young days, and unchained the door. He closed it behind him as they stepped out into the stupefying heat of the vestibule.

"Thick evening," said Gamadge, as they went down the steps and turned west. The sky there was yellow, turning to violet, to purple; no human being could be seen as far as the eye could reach, but presently they passed a caretaker sitting on the front steps of his house in his shirtsleeves, and Gamadge nodded to him.

"You never see anybody," said Idelia.

"No; it's like a plague year. The court has moved to Hoydon; somebody will write a beautiful poem about brightness falling from the air—there will be fever in it."

A commotion above made them glance upwards at a plane whose body was almost invisible; the cluster of colored lights blinked on and off, on and off, as they sailed north.

"Just a product of our fevered imagination," said Gamadge. "It will vanish. It was never really there."

Idelia said: "I like those big drugstores, with all the lights and everything to buy."

"They do give us a sense of reality. After we've been to the hospital we'll visit one; you must have a soda. I always stand a new client a drink. Hurry, Idelia; there's a bus stopping for a red light."

CHAPTER FOUR

St. Damian's

THE BUS DOOR WAS OPEN, the driver motionless at
the wheel like a wooden man. A few passengers, dummy-like
and morose, endured the journey and the gloom of the dim-
out in silence. Gamadge put the fares in the box, and followed
Idelia to the seat she had chosen next to the exit doors. The
thin four-pointed red star of the street-lamp turned to green,
and the bus began its climb uphill.

After an interval Idelia turned her head. "Mr.
Gamadge."

"Yes?"

"You said something about knowing why I couldn't get
information at the hospital."

"Knowing? It was a wisp of theory. I have them."

"Can't you tell me what it is?"

"You won't like the one that leaps to the eye."

"Why not?"

He replied with another question: "Have you ever seen a
drug addict?"

"A what?" She spoke so indignantly that he knew he did not need to answer. Presently she asked: "You mean somebody that takes morphine?"

"Or cocaine, or any narcotic drug."

"You mean Mr. *Crenshaw* was one?"

"It's a mighty good guess."

"He wasn't!"

"You know?"

"I've read about them, and I've heard about them. Mr. Crenshaw wasn't nervous or jerky. He acted quiet and natural."

"Perhaps he wasn't so quiet and natural on Sunday, when you weren't allowed to see him."

Idelia gazed at him in silence.

"You mustn't be horrified," said Gamadge. "You've engaged an investigator, and it's his duty to canvass all the possibilities and reject them one by one—until he meets one he can't reject. The drug theory answers some questions, you know."

"How does it?"

"Well, look at the situation up there in Vermont. Pike was the drug peddler who supplied Crenshaw from some distant source. If Crenshaw was frightened when Pike's car came into sight that time, he was afraid that Pike hadn't the consignment. Or he was afraid the supply mightn't be satisfactory in quality— perhaps it hadn't been, the last time. I understand that owing to war conditions bootleg drugs are much weakened by adulteration, so much so as to be practically useless to the addict.

"The addict is completely dependent on his source of supply. Crenshaw wouldn't let Pike see you because Pike wouldn't approve of his making friends; he might betray himself to them, or he might confide in them—you never can tell what an addict will do. Discovery would be a serious matter for Pike—drug traffic is a felony.

"Then look at the marked passages in the Shakespeare—this theory explains them, too; for such is the peculiar construction of weak human nature," said Gamadge, who was talking slumped down in his seat, his eyes fixed on nothing, "that it often blames the pander to its weaknesses. Crenshaw wouldn't be grateful to Pike; he'd even hate him. He'd despise him, but he'd also despise himself. Pike is born to be hanged, he himself is a monster of weakness; credulous, too, if Pike has overcharged him or deceived him about the quality of the supply.

"One day the supply doesn't come, or is useless. Crenshaw is on the point of collapse; they must pull up stakes and rush to the source—presumably New York, where a distributor has headquarters. But Crenshaw collapses at the apartment. Pike, terrified, must get him a doctor; explaining, of course, that he, Pike, is only an attendant, paid to keep Mr. Crenshaw off the stuff, unable to prevent him from getting and concealing it.

"The doctor puts Crenshaw in hospital. The hospital won't tell what Crenshaw's trouble is; the doctor won't tell, especially if the doctor—but I mustn't let my imagination run quite away with me, must I?" He looked at Idelia, smiling.

"If this is the truth of the matter," he went on, while she stared at him with round eyes, "Crenshaw didn't of course meet Pike originally in Unionboro; he brought him along from California, or picked him up in New York. Well, we have Crenshaw's isolation explained, we have Pike's terrifying quality explained—an inherent criminality that you felt rather than consciously saw—and we have the explanation for the sudden flight to New York and the isolation here. And we can understand Crenshaw's absent-mindedness; in that state he would forget his Shakespeare—and his friend."

Idelia interrupted at last, and with feeling: "You didn't know Mr. Crenshaw. He wasn't a drug fiend."

"Well," said Gamadge, "I didn't say that this theory does explain everything. Nor does the theory that Crenshaw was an alcoholic."

"He certainly was not!"

"You can't always tell by looking at them, you know."

"He wasn't any kind of an addict."

"Is Stonehill dry?" asked Gamadge, ignoring her protests.

"As a bone."

"Pike might have had bottles in that car. On July the third, Crenshaw has the beginnings of an attack of D.T.s. Pike writes to the apartment in a hurry—I wish you'd preserved that envelope; if he's a bad hat we might like to have a specimen of his handwriting—and gets the patient to New York before he crashes completely. From the sixth of July on, Crenshaw is flat on his back; acute alcoholism is no joke. Doctor, hospital, lack of bulletins to callers—all as I suggested before."

"I suppose," said Idelia with some disgust, "that alcoholics read *The Tempest*?"

"I don't know why they shouldn't. It would take them right out of this world, into a place where strange, hollow, confused sounds are mild phenomena, and mopping and mowing the order of the day."

"He wasn't an alcoholic."

"Then there's blackmail," continued Gamadge, half to himself. "In that case Crenshaw was forced to keep his blackmailer on the premises; support him as well as pay him. But we know so little; we haven't the financial picture."

"I don't believe there's anything to blackmail Mr. Crenshaw *for*," said Idelia in a kind of desperation.

"But you know that he considers himself weak, morally weak. Weak people incur blackmail, weak people submit to it. But an idea strikes me."

"Another one?" asked Idelia dryly.

"Would Crenshaw underline passages reflecting on Pike's character with Pike at his elbow? Or didn't Pike mind knowing that Crenshaw thought he was born to be hanged?"

"I don't believe that that Pike ever looked at a book, much less Shakespeare!"

"I have to take your word for so much," complained Gamadge.

Idelia looked out of the window. Gamadge, watching her stern profile, realized afresh how much her friendship with this older, literate, cultivated man must have meant to her. To defend it she had stepped right out of character. She was, Gamadge thought, the last person in the world to presume on an acquaintance and force herself where she wasn't wanted; she was convinced that Crenshaw would not have dropped her unless he had been coerced or in extremis. She was determined, in spite of her natural reticence and her acquired social humility, to find out whether he had been coerced, whether or not he was a free agent now.

Crenshaw had probably been the most interesting adventure in her life; if that was the case, Gamadge feared that her life had been and would continue to be a flattish one.

The bus, stopping for lights, stopping at every fourth corner to take on and discharge passengers, had climbed the hill and descended into the succeeding valley; now it was climbing again. Idelia turned: "We're almost there."

The bus stopped; they got out and walked through the steamy twilight along dark streets. At last they reached a corner where huge old sycamores hung their branches over a brick wall.

"I don't remember ever having seen this old place before," said Gamadge. "Or if I have, I never noticed it."

"The front entrance isn't on this avenue," said Idelia. "It's down the street."

"Shall we walk around the block first?"

"You like to start with the outsides of things, don't you?"

"Think of the things *you* buy," laughed Gamadge.

Perhaps Idelia did not realize that if they were now on very easy terms, she had Gamadge to thank for her lack of awkwardness. At any rate, she smiled up at him complacently enough as they followed the high wall up the avenue and into the next street. As they approached the end of the block they passed old wooden doors, painted green and padlocked. Within the grounds of the hospital could be seen the slate roof of a small detached building.

"The laundry?" suggested Idelia..

"Or the morgue. This must be an old foundation; Crenshaw certainly picked up an oldfashioned doctor."

The big brick hospital filled the southeast corner of the block. It was a rambling Gothic structure, with high windows, a high doorway, and a high flight of stone steps. One of the oaken doors had a bronze tablet, with *St. Damian's Hospital* in Gothic lettering; the other door was open.

"Don't we *ring*?" asked Idelia, as Gamadge urged her through into a badly lighted hall.

"Ring? At a quarter to nine?"

"It might make them mad to have us walk in."

"They'd be madder if they had to answer the bell. The hospitals haven't enough nurses at present, much less doormen."

The hall was lofty and rather narrow, with paneling of shiny yellow oak and a floor laid with red and yellow tiles. There was a bench in an alcove along the righthand wall, and farther along in the same wall an office window. Gamadge left Idelia sitting on the bench, and went up to the window. A young woman sat in the rear of the little room reading a magazine.

Gamadge tapped on the ledge.

She got up and came forward. "Yes?"

"I called to inquire after Mr. Howard Crenshaw."

"Crenshaw? Wait a minute. I just came on duty." She turned to her switchboard, hesitated, and then began to rustle through a file of memoranda. She looked up. "You a relative?"

"No. I'm inquiring on behalf of a friend."

She turned back to the file. "I remember now; here it is, I found it. Mr. Crenshaw died this morning."

Gamadge looked back over his shoulder. Idelia, sitting forward on her bench, had followed the conversation; she sat motionless for a moment or two, and then sank slowly back to lean against the wall. Her face was expressionless.

Gamadge faced the receptionist again. He said: "I'm greatly shocked to hear that. May I see someone who could give me details?"

"Just a second." The girl went into an inner office. She returned with a short, gray-haired man in spectacles, who came through a door in the partition and addressed Gamadge with interest:

"I'm really glad to meet a friend of Mr. Howard Crenshaw's."

"Friend of a friend."

"Perhaps of the lady who inquired before? Our receptionist tells me that she called last night and a week ago; described herself as a slight acquaintance, summer acquaintance."

"That's right."

The spectacled man had no view of Idelia in her alcove. He went on: "The inquiry was filed and reported to the supervisor. Even last week—within an hour of the time Mr. Crenshaw arrived at St. Damian's—he was unconscious. His doctor sent down word that he could receive no messages, and as a matter of fact he never regained consciousness again. This Miss Fisher—the name is Fisher?"

"Yes."

"We have her name and address. She left them here last week. Will you kindly inform her that Mr. Crenshaw died this morning at eight, and that the remains are at Buckley's? One of the best houses in the city. A first class undertaking firm. They are arranging to send the body up to Vermont early tomorrow, for burial there in the family plot. A little place called Stonehill."

"I'll tell her."

"We were instructed by Mr. Crenshaw himself; an unusual case, very unusual, but he was a most unusual man. I wish more were like him. Everything arranged beforehand, and paid for—down to the last penny. In cash. We have the itemized accounts, up to and including Buckley's charge for shipping the remains to Unionboro. I understand that the Stonehill people take over then. We are forwarding the accounts, with a small cash residue, to Mr. Crenshaw's bank, the Western Merchants; I understand that they have a branch, or are a branch of a bank in California. San Francisco. We notified them here at once, and San Francisco has no doubt been notified by this time."

"Mr. Crenshaw's body wasn't cremated?"

"No, and that's the only thing I can possibly criticize in the arrangements—or could, if I wished to criticize. It would have been simpler, in these days of difficult transportation; but Mr. Crenshaw said nothing about cremation."

"Who was his doctor?"

"Dr. Florian Billig. He has been associated with this hospital," said the spectacled man, "much longer than I have. I'm night superintendent, by the way; Thompson. Billig's a very good man," continued Mr. Thompson without enthusiasm. "A St. Damian's man all his professional life. General practitioner now, but at one time I believe he specialized in diagnosis."

"What did Mr. Crenshaw die of, Mr. Thompson?"

"Oh—I thought you knew. Leukemia, acute leukemia."

"Really...That's quite incurable, isn't it?"

"As yet. But you know," said Mr. Thompson with a smile, "that medical science is never at a standstill. They're working on leukemia."

"Dr. Billig diagnosed the case as leukemia?"

"Yes, just over three weeks ago. I understand that Mr. Crenshaw and his man—valet, something—arrived at Mr. Crenshaw's apartment on the afternoon of the sixth. Mr.

Crenshaw had had a sudden attack of hemorrhage in Stonehill, where he was settling an estate. You know that hemorrhage is a symptom of the disease?"

"I didn't know."

"It is. There was another attack when they reached New York, and the man was frightened; he rushed out and got the first doctor he could find—around the corner."

"Mr. Crenshaw was lucky that he got such a good one."

"Yes, indeed. Mr. Crenshaw refused treatment, wouldn't consider hospitalization until last Wednesday, the twenty-first. It's a curious disease; when he arrived here with Dr. Billig, in a cab, they tell me that he seemed quite well, except for general weakness. He settled all the affairs I mentioned, deposited the cash with us, and then—" Thompson raised his hands, and then lowered them, palms down, in a gesture of finality— "he seemed to give way. And when we did his first hemoglobin, Mr.—er—"

"Gamadge."

"—Mr. Gamadge, we were only surprised that he had kept going so long. As I said, a strange disease."

"So I have heard."

"Such imperceptible degrees of decline, such quick collapse and death. But no two cases are alike."

"From what you said about taking a hemoglobin, I gather that Mr. Crenshaw did have treatments in hospital?"

Mr. Thompson smiled. "A doctor is quite right to humor his patient, Mr. Gamadge—when the case is hopeless; but in a hospital we go on fighting for the patient's life, I'm afraid, until the end."

"X-ray treatments, all that?"

"And blood transfusions. We never give up. But if we had done nothing at all, the result would have been quite the same."

"Well, I'm infinitely obliged to you, Mr. Thompson—"

"I was going to suggest that if Miss Fisher cared to stop in this evening, Buckley's would be very glad to see her—to see any friend. They might be glad to have a little ceremony. Mr. Crenshaw was a lonely man; he had nobody. Rather a sad thing."

"I'll tell Miss Fisher."

Gamadge turned away in order to do so, and Mr. Thompson for the first time caught sight of Idelia on her bench. He paused, looked in considerable astonishment from her to Gamadge, gave it up, and with a backward glance of some perplexity removed himself from the scene.

The receptionist had settled down to her reading again; Gamadge, satisfied that she was out of earshot, sat beside Idelia and put out his hand. He touched hers in its brown fabric glove, withdrew his own, and said: "I'm sorry. But he's all right now."

Idelia's response was to turn a stony look upon him. She said "Drugs!" and repeated it. "Drugs!"

"It wasn't a bad guess."

"What is this leukemia, anyway?"

"I know a little more about it than I seemed to know; I wanted Thompson to hand out information. It's a disintegration of the white blood corpuscles, and when it's acute it's fatal."

"Are you sick a long time?"

"Not always. The length of time varies."

"Mr. Gamadge, he knew all the time that he was going to die."

"Crenshaw knew it while he was in Stonehill?"

"That's why he acted the way he did; I can see it now! As if he was done with everything."

"His doctor told them here that the first diagnosis was made by him in New York on the sixth of July."

"There's some mistake. Mr. Crenshaw knew it before. Pike was his nurse; he wasn't afraid of him, he was afraid Pike would think he was tiring himself out, talking to strangers. Perhaps he forgot how sick he was while we were talking, and when he saw Pike that reminded him—that he was going to die. No wonder he looked frightened!"

Gamadge said nothing.

"And of course he forgot all about me and the book," said Idelia. "He had that terrible attack. After he got to New York he had another. No wonder he forgot everything."

"Except business."

"Things remind you of business."

"There's one thing in favor of your theory, Idelia: *The Tempest*. It occurred to me from the first that that was just the play to take with you on a last journey. But why should Mr. Crenshaw have concealed the fact that Pike was his attendant, and told you and everyone that he had picked him up in Unionboro?"

"Perhaps he did pick him up in Unionboro. Perhaps he didn't want anybody to know how sick he was."

"Then we're dropping the inquiry?" Gamadge smiled at her. "You don't want to know why your friend underlined those passages, what your friend wrote in the margins of his Shakespeare?"

Idelia, taken aback by the reminder, said after a moment: "I forgot about them. Perhaps he rubbed them out because they were something about dying, and he didn't want me to know."

"The underlined passages weren't about dying. The first one is about hanging, but that was a kind of joke."

There was a long pause. Then Idelia said in a voice that had sunk to a whisper: "Something was wrong. What could it be?"

Gamadge replied as softly: "We might try to find out. I suppose he really did die of leukemia."

Her eyes grew rounder.

"They took tests and blood samples here—I was careful to ask. Tomorrow," said Gamadge, "I'll find out whether leukemia can be faked or induced. As for some insurance racket, we don't know whether Crenshaw was insured; but he wasn't cremated, so perhaps insurance doesn't come into it."

"I don't know what you mean."

"Say that a man named Crenshaw insures his life in favor of a man named Pike. A collaborator is found who wants his heirs provided for; in this case, a collaborator who is dying of leukemia. The collaborator is buried under the name of Crenshaw, and the real Crenshaw and his accomplices—Billig would have to be one of them—split the insurance. But in such cases there is always, or nearly always, complete destruction of the body; often by cremation."

Idelia, her face a mask of incredulity, asked: "Why?"

"Because insurance companies are skeptical and cautious, and they employ trained investigators to protect them against that very type of fraud. My friend Schenck was an insurance investigator before he joined the F.B.I. If there's the least cause for suspecting the parties, there's an investigation; the body may be exhumed, and no insurance crooks risk that."

"Mr. Gamadge," said Idelia in a violent whisper, "you can just forgot it. Mr. Crenshaw wouldn't have cheated anybody out of money, not even an insurance company."

Gamadge said: "We can prove or disprove the theory ourselves."

"We can?"

"And we're just in time. You wouldn't mind a visit to Buckley's funeral establishment? You won't mind saying goodbye to your friend?"

"I'd give anything to!"

"That's the talk; I see that you were brought up in a stern and pious school, to look your last upon the dead."

"But will they let me see him?"

"Thompson spoke as if they might. They may be very glad to see you, you know. Places like Buckley's love an identification; they know all about the insurance racket."

"But will they be open?"

"Places like Buckley's are open all night."

CHAPTER FIVE

Little Ceremony

THE RECEPTIONIST SUPPLIED Gamadge with Buckley's address, not far south and west of St. Damian's. It was a big remodeled corner house, stately and not too sad, with a columned and pedimented white doorway. It had its own garage on the side street, and there was a florist's conveniently located on its ground floor.

Idelia stopped at the florist's window. She said: "I'd like to get a few flowers."

"They're so *damned* expensive in this part of town, Idelia. Crenshaw wouldn't have wanted you to spend money on him."

"Those double petunias don't look expensive."

They weren't, because while she inspected them Gamadge engaged the clerk's eye, raised one finger, and displayed bills in his other hand. The clerk nodded, told her that the petunias would be one dollar, delivered them to her unwrapped, and then joined Gamadge in front of a floral masterpiece made of lilies and six feet high. Two more dollars changed hands.

Gamadge and Idelia walked the few steps to Buckley's vestibule, and looked through the open doors at a black-and-white hallway where an attendant in a morning coat paced thoughtfully.

"Just as if they expected us," said Idelia.

"In a sense they do. They gather all things mortal—"

"—With cold immortal hands," finished Idelia. "Mr. Crenshaw liked that poem. He often said it to me."

"Upon my word, I'm beginning to think that you were right; Crenshaw may not have known at Stonehill that he was going to die, but even if he didn't, the news can't have been much of a shock to him. The question is: was he lying to Billig about having had no former diagnosis, or did Billig know he had had one, and did Billig lie to St. Damian's?"

The attendant turned, saw them, and advanced.

"We were sent on here by St. Damian's hospital," said Gamadge. "They inform us that Buckley's has charge of funeral arrangements for the late Mr. Howard Crenshaw."

"Yes, sir." The attendant showed more than a polite interest. "You are friends of the deceased?"

"This lady knew Mr. Crenshaw."

"If you'll wait in the lounge here I'll get young Mr. Buckley down."

There was nothing funereal about the lounge, unless an etching of Ely cathedral might be considered a reminder of man's ultimate fate. Idelia sat in a chintz-covered chair, her eyes alert. Presently she said: "It's funny."

"Funny?"

"Now that he's dead they'll tell us anything."

"Now that he's dead he's safe from annoyance from us or anybody."

An elevator gate clashed, and young Mr. Buckley arrived from an inner hall. He was a personable youth, smartly but quietly dressed, dark and grave. He looked gratified.

"We're very glad indeed," he said, "to meet friends of the late Mr. Crenshaw."

Gamadge introduced himself and Idelia. "I didn't know Mr. Crenshaw," he explained, "and Miss Fisher only met him this summer; but she was greatly shocked at St. Damian's this evening to hear that he had died. She didn't know that he was seriously ill until they told her—the people at his apartment house told her—that he had been taken to a hospital."

Mr. Buckley, addressing Idelia with respectful sympathy, said that the final collapse had been sudden. "We understood," he went on, "that Mr. Crenshaw was entirely alone in the world. He never mentioned friends, so far as I know."

"I only knew him up in Vermont this summer," said Idelia.

"I see. That accounts for it. But we're very glad you *are* in the city, Miss Fisher. We always like it when friends come in. We have followed Mr. Crenshaw's instructions to the letter, and we like friends of the deceased to see what we are doing and have done. We're in communication with Stonehill, Vermont— in fact, we have paid them."

Gamadge looked politely surprised.

"Every detail," said Mr. Buckley, in reply to this, "was settled by Mr. Crenshaw before he died. His estimate was very generous. St. Damian's had an advance in cash, part of it came to us, and out of our share we have paid Stonehill. He is to be buried in the old family plot there; the sexton of the Congregational church there is attending to the funeral. It takes place day after tomorrow."

"I know that cemetery," said Idelia. "We have a plot there too."

Buckley seemed to think that this was a rather touching coincidence. He said: "They inform us that there had been no burial in the Crenshaw plot for a long time until Mr. Crenshaw's uncle was buried there last spring. The family was scattered; Mr. Crenshaw himself came from California. That—" he looked at Gamadge— "more or less explains the unusual cash arrangements made by him.

He had no legal representatives here in the east, no business representatives except the Western Merchants bank here. He didn't want
delay in settling his estate in California after his death."

"A business man indeed."

"I understand that he was once in the building business."

"The hospital told you so?"

"I think his doctor had had that information from him."

Mr. Buckley looked at the bunch of petunias in Idelia's
hand "You wished to leave these, Miss Fisher?"

"If I could."

"I was going to suggest—some people don't care to do
it—would you like to *see* Mr. Crenshaw?"

"Yes. I would."

Mr. Buckley seemed pleased. "Of course. If you'll wait a
few minutes."

He disappeared down the hall. Idelia said: "He's awfully
nice, isn't he?"

"Yes. What did I tell you? He's delighted. You will note
that although Mr. Crenshaw's body travels to Vermont by an
early morning train, and it's now nearly half past nine, the body
hasn't even yet been hermetically sealed in its coffin."

"Mr. Gamadge, that's all so silly—about its not being Mr.
Crenshaw's body at all. When could somebody else have taken
his place? Never."

"On the trip from Stonehill?"

"Why, but they must have known him at the apartment.
He engaged it himself, the last of May."

"Engaged it in person?"

Idelia was silent.

"I can find out tomorrow," said Gamadge. "But even if he did
engage it in person, how about the switch being made in the cab?"

"What cab?"

"Dr. Billig seems to have taken him to the hospital in a cab;
not an ambulance."

Idelia, looking astounded, said: "I never heard of such a—such a—"

"I really think that in any case I'd better see Dr. Billig."

Young Mr. Buckley returned, and with an added solemnity in his manner ushered them along the inner hall, through double doors, and into a kind of secular chapel. There was a dais at one end of it, but Crenshaw's draped coffin stood on its bier in the center of the tesselated floor. It might have stood there all day; if, as Gamadge suspected, it had just been wheeled in from some much smaller place, that fact was nothing against Buckley's.

Young Buckley remained in the doorway. Idelia, with Gamadge beside her, went up to the coffin and looked down at the dead face within. Then she laid the purple flowers on the more brilliant purple of the pall, and turned away. She said: "Poor Mr. Crenshaw. He looks wonderful. You wouldn't think he'd even been sick."

Buckley spoke from the doorway, in the accents of one who has received a valued compliment: "It's that disease, Miss Fisher. You wouldn't know until the very end that there was anything the matter with the patient, and nothing shows much afterwards."

Gamadge had lingered beside the coffin to study the calm, pleasant, sleeping face of the dead man. Light hair was brushed back from an intelligent forehead, the nose was fine, the mouth kind, the lower part of the face insignificant, but not noticeably weak. Crenshaw's was certainly not the face of a common swindler.

Gamadge rejoined the others. Idelia was saying: "Thank you ever so much, Mr. Buckley."

"We're always only too glad."

Buckley accompanied his visitors to the very steps of his establishment; he even stood in the light from the hall and watched them to the corner. Then he turned and went in, while Idelia gave her investigator another piece of her mind: "I hope you're satisfied!"

"Quite satisfied. It's always a satisfaction to get firsthand evidence."

"You've seen him now; can you imagine him cheating anybody out of money?"

"No; I can't. But it isn't a strong face, Idelia; he wasn't a strong character."

Idelia shifted her ground: "You didn't see him until after he was dead."

"They're off their guard when they're dead."

"He didn't seem weak to me."

"If we're right about those underlined passages he seemed weak to himself."

"You ought to have heard him talk."

"Oh, bless you, they can talk your ear off."

"Who can?"

"Those charming bookish people. I don't want to speak ill of him, but we must analyze him for good reasons of our own. According to you he was afraid of his handyman, and I'm inclined to think that your first impression about that must have been right. He was afraid to acknowledge his friendship with you, greatly as he must in his loneliness have prized it. He was afraid to get into touch with you again, to explain why he left Stonehill without a word."

"He was sick." Idelia added somberly: "I don't believe anybody ever thought as much of me as Mr. Crenshaw did."

Gamadge, looking down at her, fancied that this might be true. A flattish life, Idelia's, and he was not at all sure that it would improve with the years. She had not many resources, and her mind—respectful of great works but hardly attuned to them—was not an interesting one.

At present she looked desolate. He said: "There's one of those drugstores you like so much. You must have your soda, and then I'll see you home, and then I'll try to get hold of Billig."

"Tonight?"

He looked at his watch. "Nearly a quarter past ten; I may find him in his office yet, but if I don't I'll call him at home. Billig is our link with Crenshaw, our link with Pike; I don't want Billig forgetting details that may be valuable to us."

"If Dr. Billig killed Mr. Crenshaw, he won't forget that!"

Gamadge said, smiling: "By your expression I'm inclined to think that you don't take that theory much more seriously than I do."

"I don't believe he could fool a hospital."

"With a false case of leukemia? Nor do I; but I must make certain that he couldn't."

"I wish you'd go right up there and see him now. You don't have to see me home. If I didn't go around by myself at night," said Idelia, "I'd never get to the movies. I just take the crosstown bus. It stops quite near the block my rooming house is on." She added, as they reached the drugstore: "I haven't half thanked you, Mr. Gamadge; if it hadn't been for you I never would have got into Buckley's. I don't know why I keep arguing."

"Argument is a very good way to approach a problem. But I won't give you cause to argue with me again until I've seen Billig, and reconstructed—or tried to reconstruct—those notes of Crenshaw's."

"Mr. Gamadge—I don't know how I have the nerve to ask you—"

"Go ahead, what is it?"

"I'm just dying to know what Dr. Billig says."

"So am I. Do you want a report tonight? Is that it? I can easily telephone."

"That's the trouble." She looked up at him anxiously. "The landlady in my rooming house is very nice, but when I moved in she said she didn't want the telephone ringing late. It wakes her up, it's in the hall right outside her door. She thinks perhaps it's for her, and she gets out of bed. She wouldn't mind if I sat in the front parlor and let you in." Idelia went on hastily: "I wouldn't even suggest such a thing, but the crosstown bus—"

"I see the point," said Gamadge, "and I shall take the crosstown bus. Whatever you do, you mustn't antagonize the landlady; not on your third day of residence. I may not be so late, you know; I'll take a cab to Billig's. He's not three minutes away from here by cab, I should think."

"You're just fine."

The drugstore was well if bleakly lighted, and it was full of noise: A loud-speaker discoursed the most lugubrious swing that Gamadge had ever heard, electric fans whined overhead, a crowd of girls and young men in uniform lined the soda-counter. Glasses crashed, soda foamed; Idelia looked happier.

"You can buy everything here," she said. "Books, magazines, writing-paper—"

"And candy and crockery. And you can look in a telephone book." Gamadge bought her a soda ticket, found her a stool at the counter, and went off to consult the directory. When he came back she was imbibing a double chocolate through two straws. He took down her address, and left her gazing after him; her eyes very round, the straws looking like the pipes of Pan.

He rode up Park Avenue, got out before the cab reached the Crenshaw apartment, and walked slowly past that handsome and modern building. There was no doctor's sign in any of its ground-floor windows, or beside its smartly awninged doorway; there was none in any of its windows around the corner. He walked down the side street towards Lexington.

Beyond the apartment house there was an all-night garage, beyond that a row of houses converted into flats, beyond them a laundry, a window-cleaner's, a plumber's supply shop, a small stationer's; on Manhattan, that narrow island, many blocks decline abruptly from luxury to shabby-gentility, from that to dinginess and then to squalor.

The flat-building nearest Lexington had a sign in its bay-window: *Florian Billig, M.D. Office hours: 12-1 P.M., 8-10 P.M.* There was a light behind the doctor's curtains. From a higher window a woman and a dog leaned out to take the air; ashcans stood at the top of the area steps.

Gamadge looked up and down and across the street. Blank windows stared at him from the rooming house opposite, there was a bluish light in the inferior drugstore on the corner. A small car stood at the curb between the doctor's flat and the next one.

He lives here, thought Gamadge. No doctor would have an office here unless he lived here. And I bet Crenshaw's apartment house didn't recommend him.

There were bells and namecards in the vestibule; Gamadge went in and pushed the doctor's bell.

CHAPTER SIX

Medical

GAMADGE WAS THINKING: Can't cover up for Idelia now; he's had her address for a week, knows she called again last night. He hasn't done a thing. Perhaps I *am* crazy? The door clicked, and he went into a mustard-colored hallway. A half-glass door on the right was lettered in gold: *Florian Billig, M.D.* Before Gamadge could ring it opened.

Gamadge was face to face with a big, stooping man who looked all head and forehead; in fact, as he peered questioningly up at the visitor from yellow-brown eyes he looked rather like a buffalo. His words of greeting might have been expanded into a long, grim story: "Accident? Sudden illness?" Doctor Billig could not imagine anything short of a catastrophe bringing a caller like this one to his door.

"No; I'm sorry to disturb you so late, Doctor. I stopped in hoping to get a few details from you about the late Mr. Howard Crenshaw."

The big white face did not change, and perhaps the big, short fingers did not tighten their hold on the doorknob; certainly they grasped it firmly.

"A friend?" asked Dr. Billig, in a hoarse voice that might once have been a bass-baritone.

"I'm inquiring for a friend."

"They did say that a young woman had come to the hospital."

"Miss Fisher is a client of mine; my name's Henry Gamadge, I'm a kind of document man. People consult me about old family stuff."

Dr. Billig looked moderately interested.

"I walked up to St. Damian's with her this evening," said Gamadge. "She was greatly shocked to hear that Mr. Crenshaw had died; merely an acquaintance, you know, but those things come as a shock when you're not prepared for them. The hospital informed us that you were Mr. Crenshaw's doctor; I volunteered to call."

Billig said: "Come in." He waited until Gamadge had passed him, closed the door, and came lumbering across the room. There was power in the heavy shoulders, upon which Dr. Billig finished shrugging an alpaca coat; power in the clumsy walk. The doctor indicated a leather chair for Gamadge, and sat down in his own swivel-chair behind a desk-table in the bay of the window.

The office was lighted by one green-shaded desk lamp, and most of it was in shadow; but Gamadge could see at a glance that its furniture was too big for it; the doctor had once had a much bigger office than this. Even the threadbare carpet had been cut down to fit, and an examination table and surgical cabinet had been crowded into a corner.

The doctor spoke first: "I rather understood from Mr. Crenshaw that he had no friends—no friends in this part of the world, no close friends anywhere."

"Miss Fisher, as I said, was an acquaintance. She only met him this summer. She communicated with his apartment when she herself returned to town, and was told that he had been brought to St. Damian's. She inquired there last week and last night. Tonight, as I say, she heard that he was dead. She, too, understood that Mr. Crenshaw was alone in the world; she feels a good deal of sympathy for his case. We went down to Buckley's and saw him."

"Did you? I dare say Buckley's is adequate."

"So she thought. She thought he looked as though he had never been ill."

"That's leukemia. You know he died of acute leukemia? The disease took its normal course, if you can call anything about leukemia normal. I don't know what they would have said about it in the past; called it witchcraft, I suppose." Billig clasped his hands over his stomach and rotated his thumbs. "Do you know anything about acute leukemia, Mr. Gamadge?"

"Practically nothing."

"It comes on fast, but mildly enough; a little fever, rheumatic pains, perhaps, a feeling of lassitude. In simple and inaccurate language, the white corpuscles are breaking down; and science has no way at present of arresting the process and prolonging—much less saving—the patient's life. The patient as a rule only becomes alarmed when hemorrhage occurs—hemorrhage which may come from one or more organs. Hemorrhage was what in Mr. Crenshaw's case brought him in a hurry to New York from Vermont; the first one occurred on July the third. They arrived on the afternoon of the sixth, and Crenshaw's man had me in the apartment within the hour."

Gamadge, listening with civil interest, asked: "He didn't have to go to hospital until last week?"

Dr. Billig smiled. "He didn't *have* to go at all. When a patient has plenty of money and attendance we allow him to die as and where he likes, Mr. Gamadge. I diagnosed leukemia—or rather the pathologist at St. Damian's analyzed the blood sample for me—that same afternoon. I told him next morning."

"So soon? But I suppose the question's inane," said Gamadge. "A doctor of experience knows what he's doing."

"Mr. Crenshaw was then able to transact business and settle his affairs; he might not have been able to do so later, although in fact he did not collapse until he was actually in bed in the hospital. He had explained to me that he had nobody to act for him, and asked for the truth. He was a well-balanced, sensible man; I felt obliged to be frank with him. What a doctor of experience does know," said Billig, smiling again, "is the kind of patient he's dealing with."

Gamadge had decided that this doctor of experience was at least sixty years old. He asked: "Could Mr. Crenshaw get all the treatments at home?"

"He refused treatments of any kind; and there again, Mr. Gamadge, an incurable has the privilege—while he's a private case—of being let alone. No treatment could have saved him, as I said; or much prolonged his life. I left him in peace, and if I'm ever in his circumstances I hope somebody will do as much for me."

"Did they leave him in peace at St. Damian's, though?"

"A hospital," said Billig, his thick lips forming a smile again, "can't risk charges of neglect. Besides, if they couldn't use their acquired knowledge in a hospital they'd all die of frustration. But as I said, he collapsed very quickly in the hospital. He filled out his papers, he settled all his business with the bursar; provided them with cash for everything. Then he seemed to relax—relax utterly. Never was really conscious again. It's an unpredictable disease, except that one can safely predict death."

"He was lucky to find so humane a physician. Was it really quite by chance that he did find you, Doctor?"

"Quite, quite. He had fainted; his man rushed out, ran for a drugstore; had some notion of getting spirits of ammonia. Saw my sign, and ran in. I went around, and—well: Mr. Crenshaw and I got on. He refused to hear of another doctor. Pike—his man—seemed excellent at nursing, followed my instructions to the letter."

"Pike was a valet?"

"Oh dear no; a country fellow of some kind whom Mr. Crenshaw had met and taken a fancy to in Vermont. A paragon of rustic virtue," said Billy, raising a thick eyebrow. "So much so that he was sent to the town—Stonehill—where they had been staying, to settle accounts and close up the house there. Well, as Mr. Crenshaw had taken *me* more or less on trust," and Billig gave a snorting laugh like the bray of a bassoon, "I couldn't very well impugn his judgment where Pike was concerned. Crenshaw assured me that he was a remarkable judge of character; who was I to contradict him?"

"What did *you* think of the paragon, Doctor?" Gamadge had settled back in his springless chair like a man enjoying a conversation; he took out his cigarette case. Billig picked up a package of cigarettes from the table, and Gamadge gave him a light. Then he lighted his own cigarette, and sat waiting.

Billig smoked for awhile before he replied: "I'm not qualified to judge the type. I'm not familiar with it. To me Pike seemed a quiet, rather dour, unsuccessful small farmer or tradesman, who had lived much alone and knew how to wait on himself, and therefore on others. Very independent, in the vulgar modern sense of the word. Perfectly respectable. Quite devoted to Crenshaw in his inexpressive way. He's probably still up there, waiting for the news of Crenshaw's death—I told him it wouldn't be long—and I have no doubt he'll make a point of waiting for the funeral. I don't know when that will be."

"Buckley's said it would be the day after tomorrow." Gamadge watched the smoke rise from his cigarette. "One rather wonders how great the influence of Pike may have turned out to be—on Crenshaw's testamentary dispositions, you know. One hears of these people coming in for a lot of money, even turning up as the principal beneficiaries in a new will."

"Crenshaw's will was made; he referred jokingly to middle-western distant cousins who weren't down in it. His only relatives. I think he was the last man in the world to lose his head over an employee."

"Rather odd that he didn't communicate with these cousins, or have them notified?"

Billig moved slightly in his chair. "His bank may have had instructions. I know nothing of that. He had a man up from the Western Merchants that afternoon—the afternoon he went to the hospital."

"Then his bank at least knew that he was dying?"

"Presumably."

Dr. Billig—who was, so far as Gamadge could judge, decidedly not a meek character—had responded to what he could only have thought an inquisition meekly enough. Gamadge rose. "Don't get up, Doctor; and thank you very much for giving me this information. I'll report to Miss Fisher, and she will be gratified. And her duty towards an acquaintance whom she liked very much—and was very sorry for—will have been done."

Billig sat looking up at his guest. "I don't quite understand," he said, "how they came to meet. From what Crenshaw said, and from what I assumed, Crenshaw was already weak and ailing at Stonehill; I mean he didn't go out—hardly left the place."

"Casual thing, I believe," said Gamadge. "Miss Fisher took walks; she was accustomed to a walk that led through the old Crenshaw property; she said something about Mr. Crenshaw sitting in the orchard there."

"I see." Billig got to his feet. He accompanied Gamadge to the door of his flat, but no further; they parted courteously.

When Gamadge had left the building the doctor went hurriedly to his bay-window, pulled the dust-colored curtain aside, and watched his late visitor's progress to the Park Avenue corner. Then he darted into his bedroom—he was light on his feet, it seemed, when haste was required—came back with his felt hat on his head and a wrapped package in his hand, stuffed the package into his coat pocket, and hurried out of the flat.

He got into the car that stood just beyond the front steps, and started it with a jerk. He drove west; in the darkness of the car his face was not the face that Gamadge had seen—it was contorted with urgency, and perhaps with some fiercer emotion. The car turned down Park, passed Gamadge, and left him behind; Gamadge, walking along the other side of the street, head down and hands in his pockets, did not see it at all.

CHAPTER SEVEN

Nightmare

GAMADGE WAS WALKING because there were no cabs. He soon arrived at 86th Street, however, and waited a few minutes for the crosstown bus; Idelia, he was sure, would be glad to hear that his trip to the west side had cost him only five cents.

The bus came; he boarded it, and sat thinking about his report to his client while he travelled to Madison, down Madison, to Fifth, and into the blacker transverse of the park. What should he say to Idelia? That Dr. Billig was a man of intellect whose path in life led downward? That in spite of a vast self-control, developed through his professional life, Dr. Billig was very uneasy?

There was something against Dr. Billig: if his uneasiness had been founded on nothing more than a sense of the oddity of Crenshaw's isolation, he would have confessed to it; but he had not confessed to it. He had rather minimized that situation, he had been in a general way complimentary to Pike, his account of Pike was by no means Idelia's. One of them was wrong, and Gamadge did not think that that one was Idelia. He did not think that Dr. Billig had really missed what was, if not sinister, at least remarkable, in the personality of Crenshaw's confidential man.

But all this amounted to no more than a series of impressions: Gamadge's impression of Billig, who might after all have withheld *his* real impressions from a mere outsider—one who had no right to ask questions about Crenshaw at all; Idelia's impression of Pike, her and Gamadge's unsubstantiated theory that the underlined passages in *The Tempest* referred to Pike and to Crenshaw himself. After all, Billig was a reputable physician, if a shabby one; he was still a member of the staff of St. Damian's Hospital; and if Mr. Thompson, the night superintendent, had not seemed enthusiastic about the doctor, perhaps that was because Mr. Thompson didn't like fatness, shabbiness, and lack of professional success.

And Dr. Billig had not shown undue interest in Idelia.

Gamadge decided that he must know more about Dr. Billig, and that tomorrow he would call up his own doctor, the impressive Hamish.

The bus emerged from the park, and trundled its way along the next block. At the corner Gamadge got out. He walked up to Idelia's street, and stood looking down her block; a block inadequately lighted by its one dimmed-out lamp, and ending in the dimmed lights of the farther avenue. The rooming house was two doors from that corner, one of a double row of brownstone houses with high stoops. None showed any light; most of them were empty, or converted as Idelia's had been from private dwellings to lodgings of the cheaper class. A dark and desolate street indeed; a street that might have figured in a bad dream.

There was a dreamlike quality, too, in the stifling sensation caused by the heat; heat such as might be reflected from a metal screen. You couldn't get rid of that by waking up; you couldn't wake out of this nightmare at all. Behind it, causing the deadness and the darkness, was the black cloud of the war.

Gamadge walked along the north side of this dream street, past the wells of area and the lightless vestibules, past the little island of radiance cast by the street lamp, to Idelia's rooming house. No light here, either; or none discernible from the sidewalk. Hadn't she said she would be waiting in the front parlor? It was shuttered; perhaps her light was very dim—orders of the landlady.

He had his foot on the first step when he noticed that the front door was partly open. Chained back as his own had been this evening, for coolness? Rather dreamlike, to call at a New York brownstone house and find the front door open...Rather dreamlike to see a hat with a pink rose on it lying half way down the front steps.

He ran up to the vestibule. Idelia lay face downwards half in and half out of the doorway, her packages scattered about her, her handbag open and empty in a dark corner. She had done a lot of shopping in that drugstore—too much shopping. It had delayed her—she had been beaten down as she unlocked the door. Gamadge bent over her, sickened by shock and remorse.

He touched her hand in its fabric glove; still warm, but there could be no life in anyone whose skull was crushed like that. He straightened, glancing from the handbag to the spilled paper of candy, the bottle—broken in its wrapper—that exuded a powerful odor of citronella, the paper-covered book, the magazine, the toothbrush in its cellophane. Very ironical, these trifles; very ironical that Crenshaw had been the death of his last friend.

Gamadge pulled himself together, pushed the doorbell, and ran down the steps. He walked the few yards to the corner, and then made for the nearest subway station. At Columbus Circle he took a cab, reaching home at 11:29.

He was looking rather white and wild when he let himself into his dark house. Darkness suited him; but the reason why he did not turn the switch beside the front door was that there was another one at the back of the hall, near the coat closet and opposite the elevator. He had his hand on it, when something—some alien sound of motion from the direction of office—caused him to turn. He saw nothing, but his thought was: If he has a gun, goodnight.

His next action was automatic. He grasped and pulled the knob of the elevator door; if the elevator was there, the steel door would open. It was there. He slid into it, the door swung to behind him, and the elevator rose with its usual and dreadful deliberation.

He could hear a shaking and a fumbling below—his visitor had evidently thought that the door was a cupboard door and made of wood. The few moments of delay allowed Gamadge to reach the second floor, plunge from the elevator, and fling himself across the hall and into the library while feet still pounded on the stairs.

He slammed and locked the library door, which was of solid mahogany and had been built to last. The telephone, unfortunately, was in the hall; so he stood in the middle of the room, out of range, and shouted at the top of his voice at nothing: "Police? Radio car. Burglars," and added his name and address.

Meanwhile his eye was on the door; but there was no explosion, the lock did not burst out of it. Relieved, he went to the oldfashioned speaking tube near the mantelpiece, and pulled the handle of its bell. Presently a whistling noise reached him.

"Theodore?" Gamadge spoke low.

"Sir?" Theodore was speaking from the front basement.

"Lock yourself in, and telephone the precinct. Talk softly. Tell them to send a radio car. Don't make any noise or move out of there till the cops come; then let them in by the area."

"What is it?"

"Burglar."

Gamadge spent the next few minutes looking up road maps and timetables. By the time he had found what he wanted there was a loud knocking on the door; he threw it open to admit Theodore and a policeman. Theodore began to talk immediately and complainingly:

"No wonder you get a burglar, Mist' Gamadge; you left your office window open. That window stays locked. I don't go in there at night and lock up, how can I know you'll open it? You got a filter."

"It wasn't your fault. The filter was simply fanning in hot air. I had a client. You go down and make some mint juleps for me and for the officers," said Gamadge. "I suppose the other one's searching the house? No use. Our friend heard me pretending to bawl for the police."

Theodore retired, grumbling. The second policeman arrived, and Gamadge asked them both to come in and sit down. They were rather complimentary when he told them about the escape by elevator, but inclined to admonition. Martin the cat ran in, and one of the officers said it was too bad he wasn't a dog.

"What do you mean, too bad he isn't a dog?" Gamadge was affronted. "Oh—you mean he'd have barked at the burglar? But he'd bark at the milkman, too, wouldn't he?"

With the juleps arrived Detective-Lieutenant Durfee of Homicide. Gamadge said: "This is very nice of you; to what happy chance am I indebted?"

"I was at the station when your SOS came in," replied Durfee, sitting down and accepting a frosted glass. "It's news when you get in trouble. Catching up with you, are they?"

"What on earth do you mean, Lieutenant? I haven't an enemy in the world."

"There wasn't any burglar. What you heard was a breeze from that window you left open, blowing papers off your desk."

"What breeze?" Gamadge was fanning himself with a newspaper.

"Come on now, give us the dope. You can't get us over here on a night like this for nothing."

"As a taxpayer I'm entitled to protection."

"The department is entitled to taxpayers keeping their ground-floor windows locked. I'm glad your wife's out of town."

The radio policemen sat with their tumblers in their right hands and their cigarettes in their left hands, looking from Gamadge to Durfee and back again. They were awed by the familiarity between their superior and this citizen.

Gamadge said: "It's all the fault of the dim-out. Nobody climbs into front windows when there's any light on a street."

"We have a chance to blame a lot of hold-ups on the dim-out now," said Durfee. "They had one over on the west side just now; I caught the word at the station. Nice young woman, dentist's assistant, had her brains knocked out on her own rooming-house doorstep. And the murderer was kind enough to ring the bell."

"Ring the bell?" Gamadge stared.

"So the medical officer could get there in time to say she'd been killed within a half an hour. What we think is that it was some passer-by, who noticed the door was open and didn't want to get mixed up in the case and give evidence. But that's the way you citizens act—no sense of responsibility."

"I don't know what the passer-by could have told you more than you know now," objected Gamadge. He thought: That was cutting it fine, cutting it fine, and wondered why he himself wasn't lying dead on the rooming-house steps. He had just missed it; lucky that the killer had been so anxious to complete his job on the east side.

Durfee rose, and the others with him. "I suppose you want us to take fingerprints," he said.

"Fingerprints?"

"The ones that won't be on your window-frame and doorknobs."

"Fingerprints bore me."

"They bore us, too, but we have to go through the routine."

Gamadge, with many thanks for prompt service, showed the three out of the front door. As they were going down the steps, the youngest officer—exhilarated by his juleps and willing to ingratiate himself with his superior—clumsily remarked that this Gamadge was a jittery specimen, wasn't he?

Durfee stopped to look at him. "Who?"

"This Gamadge. Like you said when you were joking him in there."

"I was joking him. If that guy called you up," said Durfee, "it was because he was in there with a killer between him and the front door. If it wasn't for that little elevator of his, he'd be dead."

Gamadge, meanwhile, was formulating another theory to account for his escape. He had been studying the maps and timetables, and now stood beside the telephone in the hall, looking down at his cat. Martin was looking up at him, mewing silently in the plaintive way cats have: "Pity me, I'm so small."

"Pathetic little guy, aren't you?" said Gamadge. "Where were you, if I may ask, when the burglar came? Fraternizing with him, getting between his feet? Was that why he couldn't get to the office door in time to let me have it as I went past?"

Martin gave up and flung himself down on the floor.

"He couldn't have done a thing about you," mused Gamadge. "If he had, he'd have made enough noise to set me running; and he didn't want me running in the dark. Did you save my life, you dear little thing?"

Martin shot out a mighty paw and gripped the cuff of Gamadge's trousers. Gamadge shook him off by waggling that foot, and picked up the telephone.

When Mr. Robert Schenck answered, his voice was full of fury and of sleep: "Yes. Who?"

"It's Gamadge. "

"What did you wake me up for?"

"It's only half past twelve."

"I turned in early to forget the heat."

Gamadge proceeded to tell him a better way to forget the heat, and was interrupted by a cry of outrage: "I'll be damned if I will!"

"Schenck, I wouldn't ask it of you; but with this driving ban on, you're the only living soul I know who can use his car."

"I can use my car on Federal business, that's when I can use my car. What's the matter with you going up to Vermont yourself, by train?"

"I have to be in New York for a few days, and anyway the last train has gone—the 12:01 to Unionboro. I've just looked at the timetable."

"It's out of the question for me to go chasing around the country on your business."

"Isn't murder Federal business?"

"Not unless you can tie it in."

"I can tie it in."

"Who's been murdered?"

"My client; and I was nearly murdered myself. I had to call the cops," said Gamadge plaintively, "and even Durfee came."

"Thank God Mrs. Gamadge is out of town."

"So Durfee said."

"What happened, anyway?"

"My friend staged the client's murder as a hold-up, and then—thinking I didn't know about it—came along to eliminate me. I think he must have had a gun—he wouldn't risk breaking *my* skull. He found my office window open, climbed in, and discovered that I hadn't come home yet. He was waiting for me in the office; and when I did arrive, hanged if I don't think Martin got in his way. Anyhow, I heard something and managed to get into the elevator and up to the library. I yelled police, and he left."

"For Heaven's sake. So now you have to get this bird before he gets you."

"The only chance I have of clearing up the case is getting hold of this Pike in Stonehill."

"If you can't come up yourself, why don't you have Durfee call the people in Unionboro and hold him?"

"There's nothing to hold him on yet; I have nothing at all against anybody but a series of incidents; and by the time I persuaded Durfee that there was an element of cause and effect somewhere, and he persuaded his colleagues in Unionboro—or the authorities in Stonehill—Pike might be lost. He has a car. He's supposed to be staying over until Friday for a funeral, but he may not stay. I only want to know where he goes when he does leave Stonehill."

"You think trailing him is a one-man job, do you?" Gamadge had a clear vision of Schenck, red hair on end, standing indignant among his modernistic furniture.

"I thought little Boucher might go up with you—turn and turn about at the wheel; it's only a seven hour trip by car, probably less at night. Boucher would do anything for us."

"For you, you mean. You think we wouldn't have to be away more than a couple of days?"

"Pike will leave after that funeral; they're burying a man named Crenshaw, and Pike was his factotum. He's supposed to be up there in the Crenshaw house, closing it up."

"He'll love being tailed by my car with my sticker on it."

"He won't bother about your car. He hasn't the ghost of a notion that he's going to be tailed. He'll drive away quite openly. It ought to be a cinch for you and Boucher."

"Leave me out; I'm an investigator, not a detective. Boucher's the pro. And what if Pike ditches his car and takes to a train? Am I to ditch my car? All right, all right," said Schenck, in a tone of exasperation. "What's the man like?"

"You mean you'll do it? Schenck, I—"

"You knew I'd do it. You've done plenty of things for us; that part of it will be all right if you can just tie it in."

"I *can* tie it in."

"What's this man like?"

"Well, I never laid eyes on him myself, but—"

Schenck uttered a noise like a growl.

"—but I have a description. He's medium height, or tallish; thin, light-eyed, ragged brown hair, one of those brick-red permanently sunburned-looking complexions; he's supposed to be a small peddler or commission agent, and Crenshaw said he was a philosopher."

"Cracker-barrel?" asked Schenck, in a tired tone.

"I don't think he's that type at all. I rather think he's efficient and cool; a tough customer. Now here's something that will make your job easier: The old Crenshaw house is on a dead-end road, a mile or so above Stonehill. From what I make out Pike will have to drive into Stonehill to go anywhere—unless he walks over the mountains, and that's rough country. If you could put up on the edge of town—"

"Edge of town," repeated Schenck, who seemed to be making notes.

"Another thing: he's supposed to have been taxiing from Unionboro station in mid-June. You could check on that."

"Unionboro is a good-sized town, you know."

"But the other taxi people at the station would know if an outsider had been muscling in."

"How do I report?"

"Telephone."

"Was your late client a millionaire?"

"Money is no object."

Gamadge's tone made Schenck pause. Then he said:

"Oh. You feel like that? Well, let's see. Boucher and I will be on a tour—government business—and taking a short holiday in the mountains. That's in case somebody checks up on the car. I'll wake poor old Boucher up now; if you don't hear within an hour, you'll know we've started."

Gamadge said: "Schenck, I don't know how—" but he was cut off. He put the receiver down, turned, leaned back against the table, and stood with his eyes on the opposite wall, thinking.

CHAPTER EIGHT

Demolitions

NEXT MORNING AFTER BREAKFAST Gamadge called the distinguished Dr. Ethelred Hamish on the telephone. This was not as easy as it sounds; he had to be tracked from his home to the apartment of a patient who had flown down from the Adirondacks to consult him, thence to his Park Avenue office, and then to the Vandiemen Hospital. The Vandiemen Hospital put Gamadge on to Dr. Hamish's private offices, a receptionist nurse said that the doctor was just going to operate and was not available, and Dr. Hamish's special nurse said that she would speak to Dr. Hamish. At last Dr. Hamish himself roared into the telephone:

"Gamadge? If it's about Clara, let me alone. I tell you she's all right."

"It isn't about Clara."

"If you've been drafted I won't do a thing about it. Against my principles."

"I'd rather be drafted than frozen in what I am in."

Hamish abandoned humor: "Those trips must be tough."

"It's not the trips."

"But you do pick up information."

"Oh, yes; more than you'd think. I suppose you haven't time to get a little research done for me?"

"What kind of research? Toxicology? Why don't you go to a lab?"

"It's personal and delicate. Just tell me first—can you induce leukemia, or fake the signs of leukemia?"

"No, you can't. You can come pretty close to it, though."

"How?"

"Sulfa drugs; you can administer intravenously, if you like, or you can feed the victim a large white tablet. That'll disintegrate the white blood corpuscles for you."

"Well, what's the catch?"

"The catch is that unless the pathologist who sees the blood-smear is the laboratory scrubwoman, substituting for the regular pathologist who's gone to the war, a slight difference from true leukemia will be noted and duly remarked upon."

"Red, I'm greatly obliged for this information." Dr. Hamish's hair was far from red, being, in fact, as black as the raven's wing, but Red had been his name at the university where he had been Gamadge's upperclassman. His proud boast was that nobody had ever called him Ethel twice.

"You're welcome," he said. "Has somebody been trying a new method of murder?"

"No, according to you nobody has. I'm glad to have that settled. What I now want is a report on a colleague of yours, one Dr. Florian Billig; age, I should judge, about sixty; general practitioner, once a specialist in diagnosis. Connected with St. Damian's hospital."

"St. Damian's? It would be closed up now, except for the war. Not enough endowment to keep it going in these days."

"But I suppose they're still capable of diagnosing leukemia from blood-smears?"

"Even St. Damian's isn't enough of a has-been to make any mistake like that."

"And they wouldn't get the slides mixed up, I suppose?"

"How many leukemia patients do you suppose the average hospital has a week? I suppose you're asking about the acute variety." Dr. Hamish paused. Then he said: "I never heard of Dr. Florian Billig."

"I had the pleasure of meeting him last night for the first time. My impression is that he has seen better days."

"Just go carefully, will you, Gamadge? *My* impression is that you're monkeying with the buzz saw."

"But I'm so brave; not like you professional pussy-footers. How about getting something for me about this Dr. Billig?"

"It's a ticklish matter, let me tell you, checking up on another medico. I could only manage it through the records, or through somebody who happens to know him."

"I won't tell on you, old man."

"Mind you don't. I'll see what I can do, and call you."

"It's very urgent."

"It seems to be."

Gamadge rang off and called another address. He was answered by a man who sounded tough, sharp and busy. But when he heard who was telephoning, he mellowed: "Well, well, well. Coming to the professionals at last, are you, Mr. Gamadge?"

"My assistant's in the Marines, and I know I can trust any friend of Nordhall's."

"Quite a party that was, wasn't it? He was bound I should meet you. What can I do?"

"Well, I should begin by saying that my business is strictly private business. We can't let Nordhall or any other member of the police department in on this."

"You bet."

"I mean the man I want shadowed is a doctor, and if he found out, and turns out to be a reputable citizen, he might sue me for a million dollars."

"My operatives never got anybody sued yet."

"Have you some very discreet ones at liberty?"

"We have no able-bodied young men now, you don't have to be told that. I have a couple of old fellers; they're good, but they couldn't run around much; and if it's a twenty-four-hour job you ought to have three. I haven't got three."

"The man being a doctor, he'll be keeping office hours twice a day; and he'll probably be visiting hospitals a lot besides."

"That might make it easier."

'I have a little plan worked out."

"I bet you have. Can you telephone instructions, or do you want to come here and meet the fellers?"

"I'd better go there. Two o'clock?"

"Fine."

Gamadge went down to his office, unlocked the filing cabinet in which he had deposited the Crenshaw Shakespeare, and took that crumbling volume into his laboratory. He stood for a moment, a look of unutterable woe on his face, glancing about him; at the well-stocked shelves and the locked cupboards, the long tables, the sink, the groups of hooded apparatus; then he laid the book down and shut and locked the door.

When he came out, dripping hot but looking rather pleased with himself, he had the Shakespeare in one hand and a sheet of scrawled paper in the other. He went to his desk, uncovered a typewriter, and produced the following:

THE TEMPEST. ACT I., SCENE I.

Underlined passage: *Note in Margin:*
I have great comfort from this   What a rotten
fellow: methinks, he hath no   sport I am.

drowning mark upon him; his complexion is perfect gallows. Stand fast, good fate, to his hanging! make the rope of his destiny our cable, for our own doth little advantage! If he be not born to be hang'd, our case is miserable.

ACT II., SCENE II.

Underlined passages:	*Note in Margin*
...this is a very shallow monster:—...	
...a very weak monster: —...	
...a most poor credulous	Credulous? Aha!
monster: —	Cherchez la
Well drawn, Monster, in good	femme.
sooth...	

Gamadge studied this, still looking gratified. The notes were cryptic, but he had never expected more from them than a further gloss on character. He had been pleasantly surprised.

He locked them up with the Shakespeare, mounted to his bathroom, and had a shower. When he was dressed Theodore summoned him to lunch.

After lunch he took the subway down town, went into an oldfashioned office building, and had himself carried to the ninth floor. He sought and found a door marked: *Thomas F. Geegan, Inquiries.*

Mr. Geegan's office was neither large nor air conditioned, and Mr. Geegan was a fat man; he had removed his coat, collar and tie, turned up his sleeves, and provided himself with a palm-leaf fan. But he had retained his straw hat, which was on the back of his glistening bald head. Two elderly men sat tilted back against the wall. One of them, a tall thin one, looked tired; the other, who was undersized and alert, with a receding chin, reminded Gamadge of a squirrel.

Geegan said: "Mr. Gamadge, glad to see you. This is Mr. Toomey and this is Mr. Indus. These boys have never let me down in their lives—they're absolutely confidential, and there's nothing they don't know about their job. But they ain't so certain that a subject couldn't get away from them nowadays—not if he wanted to run."

Gamadge sat down and passed cigarettes. "I don't think Dr. Billig will run," he said. "I don't think it will be too hard to keep up with him. He isn't going to quit and leave town; and if he doesn't, he'll have to stick to his routine. If he saw me following him around he might be scared away, though; and he probably would see me, because I know nothing whatever about shadowing people.

"All I want is to know what he does outside of office hours; and I'll cover the chance of his pulling up stakes by leaving enough money with Mr. Geegan to pay expenses if either of you should have to follow him out of the city.

"To make things easier, I suggest that you move into a rooming house opposite his apartment. There's a 'vacant' sign hanging out, I think the vacancy is on the second floor front; those windows are shut, in spite of the weather, and there are no curtains in them."

"Furnished room?" asked Toomey, who was the tall operative.

"Furnished room. And the doctor keeps office hours from twelve noon until one, and from eight to ten in the evenings. I dare say he does a lot of work of one kind or another at St. Damian's hospital. He's a big, heavy man, not young; but he has a car. You'll have to depend on cabs, and I'm prepared to pay for them if you have to keep them waiting."

Indus said that they probably would; there weren't so many cabs around in the streets now.

"Get one before you need one, if necessary," said Gamadge.

Geegan asked: "Is he one of these crime doctors? Don't sound like it. Is he dangerous?"

"If I had proof of that, Mr. Geegan," said Gamadge, smiling, "I'd be talking to the police, not to you."

"I've been telling these boys that you follow your hunches."

"Something a little better than a hunch, Mr. Geegan. I wouldn't engage Mr. Toomey and Mr. Indus on a hunch."

"I mean you build up a case. Is it narcotic drugs?"

"I don't know. Dr. Florian Billig is a mystery."

"There won't be much mystery about him after Toomey and Indus get done with him. Toomey wants the night work; he'll report at eight in the mornings. Indus will report at eight P.M. They'll telephone you if necessary, and keep in touch with me."

"Call me at any hour of the day or night. I'm only sorry that I won't be able to get into communication with that rooming house; I don't believe that there's a telephone in the place. And now for the financial end of it." Gamadge got out his wallet.

From Geegan's office he went to a subway station. He rode to 86th Street and Lexington, walked to Park, and up to Crenshaw's apartment house. He went into the white lobby, where a doorman in a dark-blue uniform advanced to meet him.

Gamadge produced the newspaper clipping which Idelia had found in the coal-scuttle. "I came in to see whether this sublet is still available," he said.

The doorman looked at it, looked at Gamadge, and said he'd find out. He walked past the elevators into an inner lobby, and presently returned with a youngish man in conservative clothes, who looked rather bemused; he held the clipping in his hand as if it were burning his fingers.

"You wanted to rent this apartment for the remainder of the summer, sir?"

"If it's reasonable, and not too big. My name's Gamadge. We're having some decorating done in our house, and my wife and I thought we might be more comfortable here than in a hotel."

"I'm not quite sure whether it *is* available."

"Not? I understood that the party had died."

"You were a friend, Mr. Gamadge?"

"Friend of a friend," said Gamadge, feeling as though he had uttered the phrase at least fifty times in the last twenty hours.

"I'm not quite sure what Mrs. Crenshaw's plans are."

Gamadge was unable to suppress the beginnings of a start, but he did his best to recover himself. He said after a moment: "I had no idea that Mrs. Crenshaw was here."

"She flew from California as soon as she was notified of Mr. Crenshaw's death."

"Distance doesn't mean much nowadays, does it?"

"It certainly doesn't."

"What a shock for her."

The manager looked as if the shock had been for him. He said: "We had no idea Mrs. Crenshaw was coming. She's here with a niece, and at first she thought she might be staying on in the apartment—it's leased to Mr. Crenshaw until the first of October. She thought she might have a good deal of business to attend to, but now she finds that there won't be so much after all. I'll consult her and let you know."

"Fellow needs a friend," Gamadge told himself. He gave the manager his card. "I'm afraid I may disappoint you—and her," he said. "Your handsome place looks too good for the likes of me."

"The terms might be very reasonable," said the manager, in tones of more than doubt.

"Well, I've written down my telephone number. You might call me. Thank you very much."

Gamadge walked forth, somewhat dazed himself, into the hot brightness of the street. He stood for a moment or two, his hat forgotten in his hand, under the smart awning; then he beckoned a cab and drove home. He was none too soon; the telephone began to ring when he was half way up the stairs to the library. He took the rest of the flight in leaps, and arrived at the telephone panting.

"Yes?" he gasped.

"Mr. Gabbage? This is Mrs. Howard Crenshaw."

"Gamadge. Yes. Excuse me for being out of breath, Mrs. Crenshaw; I was catching the cat."

Although this frivolous explanation was intended to persuade Mrs. Crenshaw that Gamadge was in no desperate hurry to answer the telephone, he would not have made it if she had sounded like a sorrowing widow; but the high, muted, disagreeable voice in which she had mispronounced his name was not the voice of the griefstricken. Nor did its owner seem to be either civil or urbane; her response to his remark was a long, blank silence.

"Thickwitted," Gamadge told himself.

After a pause for a readjustment of her faculties she went on: "They tell me that you called about the apartment."

"I did, but I'm afraid—"

"I'd like to see you anyway, Mr. Gamadge. They seem to think that you knew my husband."

"I know somebody who knew him—slightly."

"That Miss Fisher? Did you call at the hospital with her last night?"

"Yes."

"Naturally I should like to talk to her, but I have so little time. I have reservations on the Chicago Limited this evening; it goes at six. I thought if I saw you, I might not have to call her up. I don't want to see more people than I can help. Naturally."

"You're going back so soon, Mrs. Crenshaw?"

"There's a great deal for me to attend to at home, and not much here; and it was only by the greatest piece of luck that I got that cancellation for the Limited."

"But how tiring for you."

"It isn't so bad by plane. After the Western Merchants Bank in San Francisco telephoned me yesterday morning I caught the 1:17. I got here at 1:55 today. The manager of the Western Merchants branch here is with me now. If you could come up I should be very much obliged." She added: "I don't know anybody in New York. I haven't been East in years. I didn't know my husband was ill; I'm rather bewildered."

"Have you talked to his doctor, and the people at St. Damian's hospital?"

"I've talked to the hospital; they told me about this Miss Fisher. I want to know about my husband's stay in Stonehill— and about this man Pike."

"I'll be with you in a few minutes."

There was every reason for Mrs. Crenshaw to be bewildered—bewildered to the point of delirium; but her lifeless voice had sounded cool enough. Was she thickwitted? Gamadge didn't know.

CHAPTER NINE

Business

As GAMADGE LEFT THE HOUSE he stopped to look with a burglar-conscious eye at the broad window-ledge that jutted out to the left of the front steps; it was no more than a short stride from the iron hand-rail, and there was a convenient hold in the brickwork above; one of a pair of little wall-fountains, lions' masks and shell-shaped reservoirs, that he had brought back from Europe long before. Clara had had them put up on either side of the front door, and used them for plants or ivy. They were now full of geraniums; the fluted lip of the left-hand one would help anybody, even a not very agile person, from rail to ledge.

I'm glad he didn't pull the thing out of the wall and smash it, thought Gamadge. I won't say a word to Clara. He had mentioned none of yesterday's events to her when he talked to her that morning on the telephone.

By half past three he was once more in the lobby of the apartment house; this time he was sent immediately up to the tenth floor. The house manager, an inscrutable expression on his face, stood waiting for him in an open doorway; he seemed to think that he and Gamadge were now comrades, and on confidential terms. He murmured: "Whatever you do, get it down in writing," and led the way into a large lobby and through a doorway on the right. Gamadge found himself in a big, dim, well-furnished sitting-room, with bright glazed chintz on the upholstery, and awnings in the windows. There were windowboxes full of flowers, and the rugs or carpet had been replaced for the summer by matting. A pleasant room.

A woman sat on the sofa with her back to the light; a man stood beside her. His hat and brief case were on a table near the straight chair from which he had evidently just risen. He came forward.

"Mr. Gamadge? I'm Watt, from the Western Merchants Bank. May I introduce you?"

Gamadge, shaking hands, said he might.

"Mrs. Crenshaw, this is Mr. Gamadge. Mr. Gamadge," said Watt, smiling, "is well-known to us in New York as an author and an—er—expert. You may safely follow his advice."

Gamadge murmured something.

"Thanks for coming up," said Mrs. Crenshaw. "Won't you sit down, Mr. Gamadge?"

Gamadge sat down; the apartment manager hovered in the rear.

"I hope you like what you've seen of the apartment," said Mrs. Crenshaw. "There's a big bedroom, and a fair-sized dining-room, and a kitchen and maid's room across the lobby. No guest room."

While she spoke Gamadge absorbed first impressions: a quiet woman—she sat motionless, her hands crossed on the handbag in her lap. A conventional woman—she could not have had many hours on the surface of the earth since receiving the sudden news that she was a widow, but she had already acquired the outward signs of mourning; not, of course, her black suit and hat, her black shoes, but her fine black stockings and short, black-bordered veil. A woman of perhaps forty, who was still handsome—very handsome, with a thin, unlined, unpainted face, dark hair too tightly waved, dark eyes, a thin mouth, a slightly upturned nose and a long upper lip. She had the kind of face that is closed against the world; what, he wondered, goes on behind those faces? Nothing? Or a coil of secret, pullulating thoughts?

She was self-possessed, but there was tension in her attitude; the tension of a woman who has always been dominant in her own small world, but is unsure of herself out of it. And as she talked on, she revealed herself still further; for she was garrulous about her affairs.

Been sheltered all her life, thought Gamadge. Knows nothing about business, has always depended on men. She's stunned; she's taking refuge under the nearest umbrella. Give a man a reference, and she'll take him on trust. Or does she want us to think so?

"It would be quite a bargain," she had gone on to say. "My husband didn't get it at a bargain, or at least I don't think so, but I could let you have it for less than he paid. He took it to the first of October, and they tell me that his estate is responsible. That means me; and I simply don't understand why I should have to abide by the lease, since I didn't even know he was renting an apartment."

Mr. Watt said gently: "Mr. Humbert has explained."

Mr. Humbert, the manager, now fluttered papers in his hand. "We're responsible to our tenants, Mrs. Crenshaw. It's only a sublet. They went to great expense to get it ready for summer renting."

"Yes, but I don't understand why he should have paid in advance for June and July."

"It's usual, Mrs. Crenshaw." Humbert's expression said that the present conversation showed why it was usual. "We get half the summer rent in advance, especially when there are no social references."

"Social references! He had social references at home." To this there could be no reply; and she went quickly on: "Why on earth did he take the apartment for June, since he wasn't to be here at all until July? He knew he was going up to Vermont. That was why he came East—to settle that estate in Stonehill."

Mr. Humbert fluttered his papers again. "Mr. Crenshaw wanted a place in New York to come back to; we are rather crowded in the city just now. It isn't easy to get an apartment at all."

"Perhaps that's why he took such a big one. Much too big!"

"He said he liked space; and the bigger the cooler, Mrs. Crenshaw. He came in and engaged it on May twenty-eighth, and we didn't hear from him again until the fifth of July. I have his letter here."

Gamadge, eyeing it, thought again of the Crenshaw coal-scuttle.

"It was written on the third," continued Mr. Humbert. "It says that he and his man are coming on the sixth, and asks to have the apartment ready. It says that Mr. Crenshaw was delayed in Stonehill by illness. We opened the apartment; it was in perfect order, with all the linen and silver left by our tenants. Fully stocked with everything, and all of the best. We engaged a cleaning woman; but after Mr. Crenshaw arrived his man did everything for him. The place is in apple-pie condition, and I'm only sorry, Mrs. Crenshaw, that you won't reconsider and stay on till the lease is up."

"Stay on? I have my tickets for the trip back!"

"Your niece—"

"If my niece stays, it won't be in a big housekeeping apartment. I want you to do your very best to rent it for the rest of the summer."

"We'll let you know immediately if we do. There is a small advertising charge."

"Really! In the circumstances, I should think you might pay that!"

Mr. Watt, coughing, said that it was not always easy for a tenant to understand the nature of a lease.

"Especially," retorted Mrs. Crenshaw in her dry voice, "when she hasn't signed it herself."

"Naturally," continued Mr. Watt, amiably—he was a gray, slender man, with all the polite skepticism of his calling—"all this has been most upsetting for you, Mrs. Crenshaw. You feel yourself among strangers. But you can safely leave this matter in Mr. Humbert's hands."

"But the apartment will have to wait for the money until the estate is settled, won't they?"

"They will."

"Then that's arranged. I shall want a cab early, Mr. Humbert; I shall be dropping my niece before I take my train. And we each have one bag."

Humbert, taking this as a dismissal, moved with some alacrity towards the door. But she halted him with another question: "Mr. Humbert, I understand that this man Pike went back to Stonehill?"

"The night Mr. Crenshaw left for the hospital; Wednesday, the twenty-first," said Humbert. "On the midnight train to Unionboro, I think. He left everything in perfect shape, as I said."

"But who on earth was he, and where did my husband find him? I never heard of him until now."

"Wherever he found him," said Humbert, "he was most fortunate *to* find him. A very efficient man; he must have saved your husband two, perhaps three nurses. And that," said Humbert demurely, "*would* have been a bill."

"I dare say he was paid as much as three nurses."

"He was worth it."

Humbert withdrew, and Gamadge recalled himself from rapt consideration of Mrs. Crenshaw's business instinct. Was the performance a true revelation of character, or was it the result of widow's panic, or was it put on to conceal the fact that she knew all about Pike, all about Crenshaw's illness, all about his isolated death? It might be put on, he thought; her kind of face revealed nothing, and it is not so difficult to pretend avarice.

When Humbert had gone she revealed herself still further, or (alternatively) went on with the exhibition: "I can't understand any of it. My husband wasn't a letter writer, he only wrote me one letter after he came East, and I suppose he didn't want to worry me. I hadn't the slightest idea anything was wrong. When he left he seemed perfectly well—I saw him off on the train. We don't live in San Francisco, you know, we live in a suburb called Sundown. He never travelled much. His letter was postmarked here in New York on the twenty-eighth of May, and now I understand that he never reached Stonehill until the middle of June. That's what his doctor told the hospital."

Mr. Watt uncrossed his legs, and crossed them again. He said: "We must make allowance for the fact that he was developing this fatal illness, Mrs. Crenshaw. After he took this apartment he may have felt the first effects of the leukemia, and decided to go to some resort and rest before he tackled the business in Vermont."

"He always did like to manage his own affairs in his own way, and I suppose he thought he was showing me great consideration by paying all those bills in advance, and bringing a copy of his will East with him. It's just the way it always was—he hadn't changed it at all. But I've been put in a most awkward position at home; it isn't as if we ever had a quarrel in our lives."

Watt looked sympathetic. "People do strange things when they're ill, Mrs. Crenshaw. I think you will be quite justified if you—er—give the impression at home that your husband died suddenly."

"I didn't know what *had* happened," said Mrs. Crenshaw.

"I didn't know who might have got hold of him. I was ever so much relieved when you brought me the copy of that will. But why should he have had it with him, unless he knew he was very sick?"

Gamadge volunteered a suggestion: "People take precautions when they set out on a long journey. Insurance, now; they take out insurance, and they don't tell their families."

Mrs. Crenshaw said: "There wasn't any insurance. It wasn't necessary. When he sold the old family business in 1939—and how right he was! I always said so!—he settled half the money on me. I've been independent ever since then, and now he's left me all the rest. I have no financial worries at all. Only I do wish I knew what had happened to that two thousand five hundred dollars."

Gamadge looked politely interested. Mr. Watt swung his foot. He said: "Need you worry? You have the itemized accounts for two thousand and sixty-odd; we don't know what Mr. Crenshaw's private disbursements were, but we do know that the doctor's bill and Pike's wages must have come out of the twenty-five hundred."

She turned to Gamadge. "It's the strangest thing, Mr. Gamadge. My husband told all these people—he filled it out on papers when he entered the hospital—that he had nobody in the world! Nobody! Except those distant cousins in the west, and we never saw them. If he didn't want me to worry about him, if he didn't want me coming East, that's all very well; but think how I feel now! And he drew his whole balance—four thousand five hundred and sixty-seven dollars—out of the bank, and paid for everything in advance, even the funeral; and we can't find two thousand five hundred dollars at all. We don't know what's become of it."

Watt said: "Why not go up yourself, Mrs. Crenshaw, and see Pike? There are bound to be bills up there; he'll explain them to you."

Mrs. Crenshaw said quietly: "I'm not going to Stonehill, Mr. Watt. I came to New York because I had to look into my husband's affairs. They thought in Stonehill that he wasn't married; I'm not going up there to be talked about and stared at."

Gamadge said: "Can't blame you."

"I'm going home," said Mrs. Crenshaw. "I'm letting the hospital dispose of his things—except his watch and studs, of course. I even let them keep his pigskin bags. They say that doctor is all right; I suppose he wouldn't overcharge. I hope Pike isn't walking off with more than two thousand dollars that he was entrusted with by my husband and isn't entitled to. I wonder if I oughtn't to call up this Miss Fisher after all and see what she thought of him. Did she tell you what he was like, Mr. Gamadge?"

"She never met him."

Watt said: "Our Mr. Ferris met him, you know; the day he brought up Mr. Crenshaw's bank balance."

"Oh; did he?"

"Yes. We sent Ferris up because he was with me when Mr. Crenshaw came into the bank on the twenty-eighth of May to bring us the letter from our San Francisco branch, and get his checkbook, and introduce himself. I thought him a very charming man, Mrs. Crenshaw."

"Oh; yes. He was," said Mrs. Crenshaw in her veiled voice.

"We gave him the checkbook which is now in your possession," continued Watt, "and we informed him that his deposit was arranged for, and was all ready to be drawn on; five thousand dollars. We took over the San Francisco letter with his signature, and showed him the letter they sent us, and that was all we ever saw of him down there.

"He drew checks, of course; for the advance rent here, and for various expenses. But he must have had plenty of cash with him when he left California, because he never came in for cash, or cashed checks."

"He always did carry lots of money on him," said Mrs. Crenshaw.

"Well, the next we heard from him was on the twenty-first; he telephoned to say that he was not well—we got the impression that he might be suffering from something slight, no worse than a summer cold. He said he'd changed his mind about staying in town, and that he thought he'd go home."

Mrs. Crenshaw's eyes, bright and shallow as jet, did not move from the bank manager's.

"Ferris took the telephone call," continued Watt, "and came up here as soon as he had had his lunch. He brought the money in a special case we use for that purpose. It was all in large bills, by Mr. Crenshaw's request, fifties and hundreds. Pike let him into the apartment. Ferris described Pike to me today; in the circumstances I was rather interested. Ferris says he was a rather tall, thin, 'Yankee-looking' man; whatever that may mean." Watt smiled. "He says Pike was more like a farmer than a valet, sunburned, and badly in need of a haircut. Kept pushing his hair back off his forehead—it was too long.

"Pike seemed rather easy-mannered, but he took every care of Mr. Crenshaw; and Mr. Crenshaw seemed to have the greatest confidence in him. Pike got his checkbook for him, and set up a writing-pad on his knees. Mr. Crenshaw was sitting up in bed; Ferris says he didn't look particularly ill, only tired."

"It's outrageous!" exclaimed Mrs. Crenshaw. "Only this untrained man to take care of him!"

"Oh, Ferris says he was evidently good at his job—had everything as cool and neat as possible. It was a terrible day, hotter than this, the end of that first heat wave; but Mr. Crenshaw seemed quite comfortable. He wrote out a check for the amount and handed it to Ferris, who then turned the cash over to him. Mr. Crenshaw counted it, and Pike put it away in the desk. Ferris was rather horrified at this casual way of treating the money, and suggested the safe downstairs;

I suppose there is one. Your husband laughed, and said it wouldn't be with him long."

Mrs. Crenshaw's expression did not change, her eyes did not waver. At least, thought Gamadge, she doesn't pretend feeling.

Watt ended his recital in a brisker tone: "Mr. Crenshaw then said that Pike would go back to Vermont, close up the house there, close accounts, and arrange for the property to be put on the market. You know the rest, Mrs. Crenshaw; the hospital received two thousand dollars from your husband in cash; they disbursed it as you know, and the small balance, and the sixty-odd dollars that was found in your husband's wallet, have been turned over to you. I really think that you will be wise not to disturb yourself about that extra twenty-five hundred. The doctor and Pike were certainly paid out of it, and you would have difficulty in establishing a claim to any part of it now."

He rose, Gamadge and Mrs. Crenshaw rose, and Watt picked up his brief case and his hat. Mrs. Crenshaw shook hands with him.

"I'm very much obliged to you," she said. "I can't stay on and make inquiries, because if I don't take the train this evening I won't get another reservation for two weeks. But I think I will ask Mr. Gamadge to call Miss Fisher up for me. She just might know something."

"She won't know how Mr. Crenshaw invested that twenty-five hundred, I'm afraid," said Gamadge, and Watt, with a somewhat commiserating glance at him, departed.

Mrs. Crenshaw went out of the room with him. When she came back she was accompanied by a small, dark young girl who must have been waiting in the maid's room off the kitchen.

"This is my step-niece, Mr. Gamadge," said Mrs. Crenshaw. "Lucette Daker."

Gamadge shook hands with Miss Daker. She gave the impression of being quite lovely; but the loveliness consisted of fine dark hair curling on her flawless neck, luminous eyes, and a skin whose coral tint was not applied. These might desert her when she was older; Gamadge thought that a certain quality— only to be described as magnetic—would never leave her while she lived.

She was not in mourning. Her printed dress fitted her casually—it had not cost anybody much in time or money—but it had a look of being her best. So had her brown pumps, and the little flowered hat and the checked coat which she carried with her and seemed about to put on. She raised a sad, grave face to Gamadge, and he looked down at her as gravely.

"Have you packed your bag, Lucette?" asked Mrs. Crenshaw. "I want to start early. I want to get you settled at the Y.W.C.A. before I take my train. Unless Mr. Gamadge can persuade you how foolish you will be to stay in New York."

The girl said: "I told you I wasn't going to the Y.W.C.A., Aunt Genevieve. I told you I'm going to Stonehill tonight. I have my ticket."

Mrs. Crenshaw stood looking at her in silence.

"I'm going to Uncle Howard's funeral," said Miss Daker. "I'm not going to let him be buried without anybody."

Mrs. Crenshaw said: "You seem to forget. He evidently didn't want anybody."

"It was just that he hated a fuss so. He just wanted to be let alone." Her voice trembled. Gamadge thought that she was under a great strain, and controlling herself remarkably.

Mrs. Crenshaw had self-control too, but her feelings towards her step-niece expressed themselves strongly in the sharp tones of her voice. She said: "As if I hadn't enough to worry me."

"You needn't worry about me. I'll be all right in New York," said Lucette Daker.

"You planned this before we left California. You knew I wouldn't have brought you if I hadn't thought you were coming back with me."

"I can pay you my fare, Aunt Genevieve. I would have come anyway."

"Your money won't last long here." Mrs. Crenshaw turned to Gamadge. "Have you ever in your life heard of such a thing, Mr. Gamadge? A girl of twenty-two living alone in New York and depending on some job?"

"Frankly," said Gamadge with a smile, "I have."

"Lucette hasn't even *got* a job!"

"I can get one. There are lots of jobs now."

"Some war job," said Mrs. Crenshaw. "That won't support you afterwards. You'll be writing for your fare home."

"There isn't anything in Sundown. I can't stay there now."

Mrs. Crenshaw gave her the look that the practical reserve for sentimentalists; then she turned to Gamadge. "I mustn't keep you, Mr. Gamadge," she said. "Would you just get me Miss Fisher on the telephone?"

"I can find you the number of her rooming house; but won't it be better for you to talk to her yourself?"

"I meant to."

Gamadge consulted his notebook, and then, escorted by Mrs. Crenshaw, stepped within the doorway of a big, cool bedroom. He dialled, waited for a reply, and then handed the receiver to his hostess; he was turning away, but she detained him with a gesture.

"I want Miss Fisher," she said. "Miss Idelia Fisher…On business…What?…*What?*…For Heaven's sake…When?…No, thank you."

She put the receiver down, faced Gamadge, and exclaimed: "That Fisher woman has been killed! She's dead!"

Lucette Daker came to the doorway and stood staring.

CHAPTER TEN

Sentiment

IT WAS CHARACTERISTIC of Mrs. Crenshaw's type to lose no time in pointing a moral.

"Now!" she said, in a tone of triumph. "Now you see, Lucette! Miss Fisher was robbed and murdered right on the steps of her rooming house. You'll believe me now when I keep saying that it isn't safe for you to wander around New York alone."

"People aren't murdered every single night," retorted Miss Daker. "Are they, Mr. Gamadge?"

"If they live on a lighted thoroughfare they're not likely to be murdered at all. I think Miss Fisher's place was on a dark side street. This is very bad news, Mrs. Crenshaw."

"I should think it was!" Mrs. Crenshaw's mind pursued its ant-like course. "Now I can't find out anything more about Stonehill, or what people up there thought about that Pike."

Miss Daker, leaning against the frame of the doorway, spoke without sympathy: "I could write to you. I'll see him myself, if he's at the funeral."

"You wouldn't know how to manage it or what to ask." Mrs. Crenshaw, followed by Gamadge and her step-niece, returned slowly to the sitting-room. She sank down on her settee. "I do think it's the queerest coincidence," she said. "Just like Fate. The rooming-house woman was upset—frightfully upset. She wanted me to leave my name. I rang right off; they might have put me in the papers. I can't make out anything about this Fisher girl, Mr. Gamadge. How well did my husband know her? How did they come to be so friendly?"

"They talked about books and things, as people will. He lent her a book, Mrs. Crenshaw; a book, I suppose, from your library at home; a bound volume of Shakespeare."

"So that's where it went to! I noticed the gap on the shelf right after he left. I thought it must be lying around somewhere. I couldn't imagine him taking it with him East. Where is it now?"

"As a matter of fact I have it; Miss Fisher left it with me last night; she was trying to get into touch with your husband, you know, to return it."

"Oh." Mrs. Crenshaw looked relieved.

"He left Stonehill in a great hurry, you know; because he'd been taken ill. He forgot his book, and I'm afraid he forgot Miss Fisher too."

Mrs. Crenshaw, gratified, said, "No wonder." Then she bethought herself: "It's one of a set, Mr. Gamadge; perhaps if you'd return it—"

"I'll send it on."

"The set might be worth something; you never know, with those old books."

"Well, as a matter of fact you do."

"Do? Do what?" she was puzzled.

Lucette Daker said impatiently: "People know all about old books, Aunt Genevieve; what they're worth."

"Oh."

"But I'm afraid your Shakespeare has no market value, Mrs. Crenshaw," said Gamadge. "The edition is American, and a bad period at that—1839; and the binding is in bad condition. But your husband's grandfather had his name stamped on the covers, and so you may prize it."

"I never noticed that. Perhaps you'd better send it, Mr. Gamadge, if you don't mind."

"Not at all."

"How did *you* come to meet Miss Fisher?"

Lucette said: "I think that's Mr. Gamadge's business, isn't it, Aunt Genevieve?"

Gamadge said: "Everything connected with her is of general interest now. I met her for the first time last night, when she came to me for professional advice. Came to me at night because she worked in the daytime, you know. My work brings me all sorts of clients: let us say that a lady finds a book or an autograph in the attic; it may be worth something, nothing, a great deal. You know: Button, Button, who's got the Gwinnet?"

Mrs. Crenshaw gazed at him foggily.

"She had the Shakespeare with her," continued Gamadge, "and I suggested that she leave it behind while we went to the hospital. I had business uptown myself, that's why I went too. She seemed rather lonely and unsupported; a nice, simple, unsophisticated girl. Well, the hospital told us that your husband had died, and we went to Buckley's."

"You went to Buckley's?" Mrs. Crenshaw's cold eyes expressed astonishment; Lucette Daker went over to the nearest window and stood there, looking down at the burning scarlet of the geraniums in the window box.

"Yes. She had the impression that everybody had, you know, Mrs. Crenshaw; that your husband was alone in the world. She was oldfashioned and punctilious. She even bought him flowers."

Mrs. Crenshaw said in a low voice: "Inhuman."

Gamadge raised his eyebrows.

"What he did to me," said Mrs. Crenshaw. "The position he's put me in."

Lucette Daker spoke in a choking voice: "He was too sick to think of that. He was always kind."

"Kind? Kind?"

"At least," continued Gamadge, "you may feel sure that Buckley's fulfilled their end of the contract. I saw him. He hadn't suffered much, Mrs. Crenshaw. He was pale, of course; but I think that was his natural coloring. Fair hair, white skin."

Mrs. Crenshaw said something inarticulate. Then she turned to look at her niece. "You pretend to think so much of him," she said. "How would he have liked your leaving me and coming here and looking for work? You need never work. You never have."

"I'm only trying to be independent," replied Lucette, in the soft voice that was too sweet to be a drawl. "You've taken care of me long enough. It isn't that I'm ungrateful, Aunt Genevieve."

"Your uncle wouldn't have liked it."

"He wouldn't have minded."

"I know what your uncle would have minded and what he would not have minded better than you do." Lucette's expression seemed to query this statement. "And where are you going to stay," asked Mrs. Crenshaw, "since the Y.W.C.A. isn't lively enough for you?"

"The Fontainebleau."

"The Fontainebleau! Your money won't last long there."

"It can't be so very expensive; it's full of girls earning salaries."

"From what I've heard it's full of all kinds of queer people. What was it Mrs. Osterley's daughter was telling us, about a girl nearly getting boiled in a bathtub?"

To save his life Gamadge could not have helped smiling; and Lucette Daker's coral lips quivered. Two charming dents, not quite dimples, appeared for a moment in her cheeks.

"And what," continued Mrs. Crenshaw, oblivious, "are you going to do until your midnight train goes? Sit in the station? You can't stay here; I want it to be ready for inspection, if tenants come."

Gamadge said with some diffidence that he would be glad to take charge of Miss Daker. "I'll see that she gets some dinner," he added, "and we might take in a movie."

Lucette glanced at him shyly from beneath long lashes. She said: "I *would* like to see Radio City." She was well used, Gamadge thought, to such offers from the opposite sex.

He seemed to have inspired Mrs. Crenshaw with ill-deserved confidence. "Very kind of you," she said.

"Then what if we start off now? Miss Daker might like to see something of New York by daylight."

"I'm ready." She ran out of the room to get her bag, and Mrs. Crenshaw looked after her with a frown.

"These young people," she said. "I don't like it."

"She'll probably be all right here, Mrs. Crenshaw."

"It's very selfish of her. I took her in when my sister died; my step-sister—I had no obligation. That was six years ago, and Lucette was only sixteen. My husband let me send her to a good school; there was no question of her earning her living."

"Perhaps that was the trouble. They get restless, especially in these times, when they haven't enough to do."

"Yes, and now the boys are all going away or gone. There really isn't much for her to do in Sundown, I suppose, but she seemed well enough contented until now. It's a nice little suburb, such lovely people, and plenty of war work."

"Shall you be staying there now?"

"Yes, but I'll move into a smaller house. There's one for sale—a little modern house that I simply love. It will be just right for me, if Lucette really insists on staying away. Do you suppose she *will* get work of some kind, Mr. Gamadge?"

"Not a doubt of it."

"She may not stay when she finds out what work is really like. If she comes back I shall take her in, of course."

"Has she—did your husband leave her anything in his will, if I may ask?"

"Oh, goodness, no—that will was made before he ever heard of her. She has a few hundreds from her father. She actually ran out and cashed a check for it before we took our train. And never said one word to me until we were practically here. That's very sly."

"At that age they take a lot for granted."

"Mr. Gamadge—I wonder whether there can't have been some mistake about letters. My husband's letters."

"Some mistake?"

"This man Pike may have forgotten to mail a letter. I can't—I simply cannot believe that my husband meant to do such a thing as this to me. It doesn't make sense."

Gamadge met her eyes, and after a moment she turned her head away.

"It doesn't make sense," she repeated, less firmly.

Lucette Daker came back, her little flower-hat on her head, her coat on her arm, her dressing-bag in her hand. Gamadge took the bag from her, shook hands with Mrs. Crenshaw, and went out into the hall. Presently Lucette joined him, looking angry, and they stood in silence until the elevator came. When they were at last in the lobby downstairs, she spoke: "Aunt Genevieve is glad I'm not going back."

"But she won't admit it," said Gamadge, "to her dying day."

The manager, Mr. Humbert, took Gamadge aside.

"The young lady isn't going back to California?"

"No."

"I don't blame her."

"Don't let us forget," said Gamadge with a smile, "that the aunt has had a shock."

"At first I thought myself that she'd had a raw deal; but now I've changed my mind. I don't blame her husband for grabbing his chance to die in peace. Imagine her at your deathbed, beating down the doctor and getting advance discounts from the drugstore and the undertaker!"

"Talking of doctors, was the doctor with Mr. Crenshaw when they left here for the hospital?"

"Right on the job; I saw them off in the cab myself, with Pike standing beside me. Crenshaw wouldn't let him come along; he went back up to the apartment, and he didn't say a word to me; but I could see that he was all broken up."

"Good sort, was he?"

"Kind of a rough diamond, no real training; but worth his weight in gold to us. We're desperate for service sometimes. Of course Pike didn't know any better than to run out that first afternoon and pick up the first doctor he saw—off the street, you might say. We could have recommended plenty. The doctor was a queer old guy, not our class, but it turns out that he knew what he was about after all. Excuse me for keeping you."

"Not at all," said Gamadge, his eye on Lucette Daker; she was standing out in front, under the awning, talking to the old doorman—a little figure of liberty. With her fluttering skirts and her fluttering curly hair she looked free as a bird.

"I wanted to ask your advice. Old Mulqueen, our night man—there he is now, talking to Miss Daker; nice old guy—informed me when he came on duty and heard about Mrs. Crenshaw's arrival that there was a telephone call for Mr. Crenshaw about two weeks ago, and another the evening Mr. Crenshaw went to the hospital. We have no switchboard—our tenants all have their telephones; but we're down in the book under our city address, of course, and once in a while somebody gets in touch with a tenant that way. But we had strict orders from Mr. Crenshaw—through Pike—not to ring the apartment; Mr. Crenshaw being sick. Mulqueen just told the party—some woman—that he couldn't make the connection. All she had to do was write, you know. The second time, he said Mr. Crenshaw had gone to St. Damian's.

"He thought nothing of it. They have a lot of new girls now in drugstores and business offices, and he thought it might be one of them, calling up about some package or something. That's what she sounded like to Mulqueen, and it's hard to fool an old Irishman about voices.

"Well, now there's all this new excitement about Mr. Crenshaw having a wife, and lots of people belonging to him after all. It's the darndest thing; I can't understand it myself. Mulqueen remembered the telephone calls and got worried; should he report them to Mrs.? And if he does, will she kick up a row because poor Mulqueen didn't get the name or take a message?"

"I know what those calls were about," said Gamadge. "You needn't worry. I've already discussed the matter with Mrs. Crenshaw."

Humbert looked relieved. "Thanks very much. I'll tell Mulqueen. To tell you the truth, I don't want any more dealings with that lady upstairs than I can help, and I'm glad she isn't staying on. I hope we'll collect the rest of the summer rent from Mr. Crenshaw's estate; it isn't worth a lawsuit. Our tenants signed the lease, but of course we feel responsible as agents—morally responsible."

"You'll collect; Crenshaw seems to have had plenty of money."

"But wouldn't you think the widow would put her hand in her pocket?"

"That's not the automatic gesture nowadays."

"How right you are; but Crenshaw was a gentleman."

Gamadge joined Miss Daker, with apologies for keeping her, and asked Mulqueen to call a cab. It was—rather to

Gamadge's disgust—a Skyview; he objected to glare. But Lucette Daker liked it; she sat up alertly, gazing from right to left, heedless of the fact that the breeze was lifting the dark curls on her neck. They would fall into place again; they were natural curls, and she didn't have to think of them.

"How about taking your bag down to the station now and checking it?" suggested Gamadge. "Then you won't have to bother with it again until you're ready to take your train."

Miss Daker approved.

"And I can telephone. I ought to telephone home and tell my man where to find me. I'm rather expecting an out-of-town call."

"Why didn't you telephone from the apartment, Mr. Gamadge? Or didn't you think of it then? It would have been so much more convenient for you."

"Well, I hardly liked to use your telephone on my private business."

They checked the bag, and Gamadge telephoned from the nearest booth. When he came out she asked: "Where did you say they *could* find you?"

"That's a secret." He smiled at her. "I thought that we might begin our travels by walking up to Rockefeller Center."

"I'd love to walk." But as they left the station and dodged their way across Vanderbilt Avenue she seemed doubtful and a little worried. They went on to Fifth Avenue in silence, Gamadge taking profile views of her quaintly tilted nose and the curve of her round chin.

When they turned up the Avenue, she said in the soft voice that was sweetly lingering, but not quite a drawl: "You're awfully kind to do all this for me, Mr. Gamadge."

"I like doing it." He wondered what she would say if he confessed how highly gratified he was to have a key witness all to himself.

She went on: "I ought to tell you a lot of things. I ought to explain about my not going back to California, and then you won't think I'm so selfish. I couldn't stay in Sundown without Uncle Howard."

"So I gathered."

"Perhaps it's mean of me not to be more grateful to my aunt; she did take me in, and she kept me all those years; but she only does things like that because she thinks she ought to."

"Or because other people may think she ought to?"

She looked up at him. "Those people in Sundown! There's just one way of doing things in Sundown."

"I bet."

"If anybody visits there from somewhere else they can't bear it if she's different. My mother used to laugh about it. I never thought I'd have to live all my life in that place. I can't. Not with *her*."

"It must be very humiliating for her now to go back there and explain."

"That's all Uncle Howard's death is to her—humiliating. She doesn't think of *him*. She didn't understand him at all."

"What he did takes a dickens of a lot of understanding, Miss Daker."

"I know why he did it; he couldn't face the fuss, and the telegrams, and the tickets and planes and specialists. The hypocrisy! All just for appearances."

Gamadge asked after a moment: "Didn't they get on?"

"Oh, yes! They got on! You couldn't quarrel with Uncle Howard, and she doesn't quarrel either; she's above it!"

"Oh dear."

"It was just deadening to live with."

"Well, you've made your strike for liberty."

"Uncle Howard wouldn't blame me if he knew. He liked fun. He liked queer characters. I suppose that's why he liked that man—that Pike; and Miss Fisher. Was she a character?"

"Decidedly a character."

"I could see that you felt badly when you heard she'd been killed in that horrible way; but Aunt Genevieve never noticed how you felt. She never notices how anybody feels. Mr. Gamadge...'

"Yes?"

"It was queer—her being killed that very same night; the night of the day Uncle Howard died. Wasn't it?"

"Very."

"But there *are* a good many hold-ups?"

"Unfortunately."

They walked on. Suddenly she said: "Mr. Gamadge, I don't know what you'll think of me. I've been very deceitful."

"How so?"

"I don't believe you'll be shocked at me. I don't believe you'll tell."

"Try me."

"The reason I came East was because I have a friend here."

"Have you? Good."

"In the Brooklyn Navy Yard."

"Better and better."

"He's only a sailor, but he's going to be a radio officer soon. He was only a radio man in Sundown, and Aunt Genevieve didn't know I even knew him; she wouldn't have let me have him in the house. I met him at a movie," said Miss Daker rapidly, "and we used to sit in drugstores; different drugstores. His name's Judd Binney."

"No bars in Sundown?"

"He wouldn't have taken me into a bar. He's an awfully nice boy, and so clever. He's had a very good education."

"High school?"

"He started to work his way through college, but he couldn't manage it—he had family dependent on him. So he started out in the radio business for himself, and then the war came."

"And you telegraphed him that you were coming to New York?"

"You think I'm awful, Mr. Gamadge, but it was our only chance. He's going off somewhere with his ship next week. When he gets back we'll be married; I'll just fade out."

"But not too suddenly, or Mrs. Crenshaw will put the police on you."

"Oh, she won't care; she'll never bother about me again if I write that I'm married."

"How will you be off for money until your friend gets back? Or will he share his pay with you?"

"I don't need it. I have six hundred dollars."

"Too bad you have to sacrifice your expectations from your aunt."

"I can't help it."

"How much has she, if I may ask? Do you know?"

"Uncle Howard told me once that after he sold the business he settled a hundred and fifty thousand on her, and kept the same for himself."

"And now she gets the other half too?"

"I suppose so."

"Why did he make the settlement on her, I wonder?"

"Because he wanted to feel free to do what he liked with his own money and spend it any way he wanted, and not have her nagging at him and asking him questions."

"Too bad you're giving up your share of the money; I suppose you are."

"She'll never give me anything now, or leave me anything; but I don't *care*, Mr. Gamadge. Mr. Gamadge, you don't think I'm doing the right thing."

Gamadge, feeling somewhat trammeled and bogged down by so much virtue, said that he couldn't criticize Mr. Binney or herself for unworldliness. "But you're rather young to plunge into this marriage, you know. Are you sure you're not doing it just to get away from Sundown, California?"

"I'm sure!"

"You'll have lots of other chances if you wait, you know. You'll meet lots of other men."

"I know I'll never meet anybody like him."

"You've planned to meet him at Radio City?" Gamadge smiled at her.

"On Sixth Avenue. There's a cafeteria there he likes to have dinner in."

"What time?"

"Half past six."

Gamadge, having repressed a slight moan, asked her if she wished him to disappear before Mr. Binney arrived. "Oh, no; I'd like you to meet him."

"Well, we have lots of time for a cocktail first. It's only a quarter to six."

"Where?"

"I'll show you."

They had reached 49th Street, and Gamadge took her along the Avenue to the middle of the next block, and asked her to look across the way. He himself stood with his head back, gazing at the great shafts that drove up into the sky. He said: "Isn't it lovely?"

"Lovely?" she looked up too. "It's so plain!"

"Very plain."

They crossed the street, and she looked down the long vista of flowers and fountains. "Is that statue down there the one they make all the jokes about?"

"Yes. Don't you care for our gold man, Miss Daker?"

"I thought everybody made fun of it."

"It certainly wouldn't do to be too solemn about him. We'll have our cocktails down there under the awning."

"Right out doors? How wonderful!"

"Only it isn't as gay this summer as it was last summer."

"I think it's lovely. Did you tell them to call you on the telephone *there*?"

"If my call came. Now I won't have to tell them to call me somewhere else later, shall I?"

"Oh dear, I haven't treated you very politely! But I don't think," said Lucette, smiling up at him, "that it will be much of a hardship for you to miss spending the whole evening till twelve o'clock with me!"

They descended the slope. At approximately that moment Mrs. Howard Crenshaw should have been descending another slope—the ramp at the Grand Central Station which led passengers to the Century Limited. But she was doing no such thing. She had been put into her cab at five thirty by Mr. Humbert and Mulqueen, her bag, duly labelled, had been put in beside her, and she had been driven down to the station. But when the Century rolled out at six o'clock she was not on it; she was not in the terminus at all.

CHAPTER ELEVEN

Burn the Book

GAMADGE AND LUCETTE DAKER found a table under the awning of the Grill Bordeaux. Gamadge, laughing, put her with her back to Prometheus, since she didn't care for him, and faced the west himself. Lucette had a splendid view of all the other people at the tables, a view she appreciated vocally.

"I have too many flowers in my hat!"

"Is three too many?" Gamadge looked at the "hat," which consisted of the three flowers, and—so far as he could judge—nothing else.

"They only have one."

"Why any?"

"Just to show they're not at home!"

"That's putting the finger on it."

He had ordered an oldfashioned for Lucette, since she said she was used to them, and a Martini for himself.

When the drinks and the canapes came, Lucette remarked that Uncle Howard always said good Bourbon couldn't hurt you.

"Did Mrs. Crenshaw always say so too?"

"She doesn't drink."

"What a woman."

"Mr. Gamadge, you think I'm awful about her; but it's just that I can't bear people who never say or do anything they mean. For instance she puts brown rinse on her hair."

"Without meaning to?"

"Of course she means to. They do it at the hairdressers' whenever she has a shampoo. At first she said she didn't know they were doing it, and then—when her hair got too gray for her to pretend any longer—she said it wasn't a dye because it washes off!"

"Disingenuous of her, very."

"*She* doesn't need oldfashioneds; she's oldfashioned enough herself."

"That is unworthy of you; and I don't mean morally."

Miss Daker laughed.

"But to be oldfashioned, in your sense," continued Gamadge, "doesn't mean to be without emotion, you know. Far from it. People may have lots of emotions, repress them rigorously, and call it self-control—a quality once highly thought of."

"I don't think Aunt Genevieve has any emotions."

"You mustn't be too sure."

Lucette Daker took a sip of her oldfashioned. Then she said in a thoughtful tone: "I know her pretty well."

"Do you? So her friends in Sundown would say; but their judgment of her wouldn't be yours."

"*They* don't know her!"

Lucette Daker had emotions, and just now they were getting a little the better of her; Gamadge, seeing that she was trembling slightly, called for the check. "Mustn't keep Binney waiting."

They went through 49th Street to Sixth Avenue. A young, stockily built man in white, with his sailor's cap on the side of his cropped head, started eagerly forward as they turned the corner. Ignoring Gamadge, he advanced to seize Lucette by the arm, just above her elbow. "You got here, kid!"

"Yes, Judd, here I am." She gently freed herself from what Gamadge thought of as the grip populi. "I want to introduce you to Mr. Gamadge. He's been awfully kind, and I told him all about us and everything."

Binney looked up, nodded, and said: "Thanks." Gamadge's presence evidently did no worse than bore him; this thirty-seven-year-old civilian could be no more to his loved one than a mentor, and not a permanent one at that. But Binney's expression was not hospitable.

"Very glad to make your acquaintance, sir," said Gamadge. "I'll have to be running along, now; I see I'm leaving Miss Daker in good hands."

He looked back once; Lucette was being firmly propelled into the cafeteria.

When he reached home he had his bath and shower, and then—observing from the library window that Theodore had just watered down the yard, and that a pleasant smell of wet leaves and grass arose from it—he rounded up Martin for what he persisted in calling a stroll in the shrubbery.

For him this meant adjusting Martin's harness, snapping on the leash, putting his hand through its loop, and sinking the hand in his pocket. He would then wander thoughtfully along the paths and around the tree, pausing to inspect the privet and forsythia, the niche and fountain built into the brick wall, the condition of the turf, and the paint-work on the white iron garden-furniture. Meanwhile, forgetting Martin entirely, he would pay not the slightest attention to him.

Martin's procedure was also invariable; incapable of learning the uses of leash and harness, he always began the alleged stroll by gambolling like a kitten; but at the first hint of restraint he would lie down, seize the leash in both paws, and playfully chew and worry it. He would then find himself sliding along on his back, spring up in a rage, bolt off, bring himself up short, and cast himself down again for another bout with the enemy.

Theodore had never approved of the strolls in the shrubbery. On the present occasion he came to the back door and stood frowning. He said: "That cat goin' to break his back some day, tryin' to keep up with you."

"Trying to what?" Gamadge turned to look down at his pet.

"His supper's ready."

"Take him away. "

Theodore gathered Martin into his arms. Gamadge added: "I'll have my supper out here tonight. It's much cooler than it was."

"You is so overlooked."

"Let 'em look. Those fellows in the Charter Club will jump out of the windows when they smell my dinner."

Theodore was not appeased. He remarked carelessly: "Long distance for you on the wire."

Gamadge, with a howl of rage, sped into the house and up to the office. "Schenck? I've been half crazy."

"Never got a minute till now. I couldn't risk leaving the lookout. But a few minutes ago I saw Pike driving past with two men, headed for the Crenshaw house. He drove in to get them. He's boarding up tomorrow, and one of the men's insurance, and the other real estate. They're giving the place a once-over. Going to try to sell. I walked up that way myself while Boucher was having his dinner—in a front window of our boardinghouse—and let me tell you that the Crenshaw house will be a haunted house in a couple of years."

"Why?"

"Because nobody *will* buy it, and it's up there all by itself on a lonely road, and the grass will get tall, and the paint will come off, and birds and animals will get in there. Somebody'll hear a noise, goodbye."

"You don't like the place?"

"I don't like any deserted place, city or country. Do you?"

"Well, thank goodness you got there, anyhow."

"Oh, yes. We rolled in at a little after nine this morning—into Unionboro, I mean. Boucher driving, me asleep. Now don't interrupt me; I arranged for time with the Unionboro operator, but we mustn't outstay our welcome."

"While you give me word-paintings of haunted houses."

"Thought you'd want to know what the Crenshaw house is like. It's a plain, not very big farm; dooryard in front with maples; side yard with oaks and elms; grass poor; orchard sloping up back, stone wall—"

"I get it. Skip that."

"Whatever you say. To start at the start, we made inquiries at Unionboro Station; nobody at all, no outsider, did any hauling there in June. That's final, and that means Pike was lying about it.

"We then drove up to Stonehill, nice little place, but it has a network of roads leading out of it. We never could have kept an eye on Pike if we hadn't found a boardinghouse—terrible, too—on the edge of town. Pike has to drive past every time he comes in. We got two front rooms upstairs.

"Boucher's been asleep all afternoon. I turn in right after supper, but I'm going to make him wake me early, because he's got to have another nap tomorrow morning. We're both going to be on hand for the funeral, which is scheduled for two o'clock; we think our friend means to leave for good soon afterwards.

"We saw him before we ever got our rooms in the boardinghouse; when we stopped at the post-office on our way through, to plant our story and pretend to arrange for mail. I went into the post-office; Boucher stayed in the car; Pike is never to get a look at Boucher, because if we have to split up Boucher will do the actual trailing.

"Pike looked regular to me, I'll say that; gawky type, sunburned, light eyes, hair cut with the garden clipper—you know; home style. Old suit and shirt, no hat. His car's an old Ford sedan. He was in the newspaper store next door to the post-office; post mistress says he came up from New York on the night express, morning of July twenty-second; stopped around paying bills and getting stores for himself. Told about Crenshaw being taken to the hospital, and showed a letter to the bank and other people, authorizing him to close the house up.

"Boucher says he *isn't* regular; says he's a fake. He didn't get a close view, but he sticks to it that he's no small-timer. Says he's an enigmatic individual and a droll type."

Gamadge put in his first word: "Mystery man, is he?"

"So Boucher says. Something in his walk, something in his eye, something Boucher can't put the finger on. Boucher's the pro, he chased plenty of types, when he was with the Sûreté; but I don't pretend to get these nuances," said Schenck, putting three syllables into the last word.

"For the record," he went on: "Pike and Crenshaw arrived here in Pike's car on the fifteenth of June; might easily have landed at Unionboro that morning by the night express, getting in at 8:52. I'm checking up on the car—we have the number, of course. Might as well find out whether they picked it up in Unionboro that morning, where Pike bought it and when; *if* we can find out, you know. If he did acquire it lately, and in this vicinity, we have a chance.

"They lived up at the Crenshaw place until the morning of July sixth, when they took the day express down to New York. They were seen taking it. Pike garaged the car in Unionboro, small place away from the station.

"Pike came back at 8:52 on Thursday, the twenty-second, as I said. He's been up at the house since. Working hard, leaving it better than he found it. He didn't act surprised yesterday when he heard at the post-office that Crenshaw was dead; said he expected it. Acted exactly right; they all think he thought a lot of Crenshaw.

"Last news off the wire: Crenshaw's body arrived at Unionboro late this afternoon, came up on the day train. Is now at the undertaker's in Stonehill. The Presbyterian minister will conduct a small service at the graveside. He's had his fee."

Gamadge spoke again: "Mr. Crenshaw was very particular about financial matters."

"So it seems." Schenck added: "The village is going to turn out for the funeral; the general feeling is that it's up to them; this Crenshaw of yours didn't have a soul in the world."

"He had a step-niece by marriage, who will attend the obsequies."

"No!"

"And he had a wife, who will not."

"Well, I never."

"The step-niece, Miss Lucette Daker, will have a word with Pike."

"Quite a surprise for him. Would you like Boucher and me to keep an eye on her? He won't drive her over a cliff, or anything?"

"There's no reason why he should. Keep your eye on him, don't waste time on Miss Daker."

"The big excitement here isn't the Crenshaw funeral, you know."

"Isn't it?"

"No," said Schenck, in a peculiar tone. "It's the other funeral, the one that's coming off next week. A Miss Idelia Fisher, old Stonehill family, she'd just been summering with her aunt here. Died the night of the day Crenshaw did. In a hold-up. What do you know about that?"

"Odd," said Gamadge.

"We think so. But of course Miss Fisher's death doesn't interest you? It must have happened a short time before you telephoned me last night."

"Lots of hold-ups nowadays."

"As you say. Well, to close up: Boucher says Pike's abso-lutely peaceful in his mind, hasn't a notion that anybody's interested in him. We've made the best arrangements we can in the circumstances for following him up; Mrs. Much, our landlady, is paid for tomorrow in advance, our bags will be in the car, but we won't go to the funeral together. It's a nice cemetery, very old, on the north side of town. Boucher will stop on the byroad with the car, and I'll sit on the stone wall, to the east. Curiosity seekers. Our one hope is that Pike won't be able to get very far with the gas shortage on, and will take a train at Unionboro. We'll take it too. But Boucher says to warn you; he's a smart guy, and we may easily run into a snag."

"Schenck, I knew you'd do the thing the right way. I can't thank either of you; you know that."

"Cut it out. You've done us favors, and all Boucher thinks of is how you finally found out what prison camp his grandson's in. If you could come up it would be simpler."

"I can't yet; I'm on this end of the job."

"Well, be calling you."

Gamadge had no sooner put the receiver down than he was rung again. This time by Dr. Ethelred Hamish. He said: "I have some information for you."

"Already?"

"It's knowing where to ask. Three people contributed. Your friend the doctor in question is sixty-three years of age, born in New York City of obscure parents, got his medical degree at P. & S., interned at St. Damian's. He showed great promise as a young man, but that's all he did have; no friends, no money, no background. No social connections at all. Married early, but lost his wife somehow—death or divorce, I don't know—such ages ago that nobody thinks of him as anything but a bachelor.

"In spite of his talents he didn't get on. It's tough in this town for an M.D. with nothing but talent. Trouble is—one trouble—he hasn't a winning personality. Isn't popular at St. Damian's. Hasn't much of a private practice now, either. Nothing in the world against him."

"Thanks, Red."

"Oh—I called St. Damian's about a very interesting case of acute leukemia they had there."

"Did you, though?"

"Only case of leukemia they ever had there. They didn't make any mistakes, Henry."

"From what you said before I thought they hadn't."

"If you have any further fancies in the matter I'll be glad to hear them."

"The only possible question in my mind now is whether a narcotic drug case, complicated by leukemia, would go down in their records as leukemia and nothing else."

"They'd have mentioned that complication to *me*."

"Of course. Thank you. I may call up again."

"Do. I'd like to be in on your investigation; if there's any such question as you imply concerning a medical man, the Association wants to know it."

"Don't talk to anybody until I give you leave, Red, for Heaven's sake."

Dr. Hamish said stiffly that he knew when to keep his mouth shut as well as the next man did.

Gamadge had his dinner in the grassy confines of his back yard, and no member of the Charter Club hurtled down to interrupt him; although he was able to wave with condescension to an acquaintance who leaned over the rail of the club terrace, four stories above, and stabbed hopefully towards Gamadge's bottle of pre-war whiskey with a long cigar.

A Mr. Indus was announced. Gamadge had him out to coffee.

Indus stood taking in the scene; then he turned to gaze up at the gray-painted brick house, with the ornamental balcony jutting from the library window. He said: "Pretty much as it always was?"

"Well, not quite. My ancestors would have thought it rather sordid of me to eat in the library and the back yard, and mix chemicals in the dining-room."

"You come down, I come up," said Indus. "My ancestors would have thought I was in clover in my room and bath." He sat down. "Here's my report: Billig got up late, took in his paper and milk at ten o'clock. Looked kind of yellow. Drove himself down to St. Damian's hospital where he stayed till a quarter to twelve. Came back and saw patients till half past one. Patients were all from what you might call the humbler walks of life."

"I might," said Gamadge, pouring Indus his coffee. "But I wouldn't."

"Anyhow, they were all men, one of 'em on crutches. All compensation cases, I should think, by the way they banged in as if the place belonged to 'em; all but one, and he had a mouse."

"A...? Oh. Yes."

"At one-thirty Billig came out and walked to an automat on Lexington, where he had lunch. After lunch he drove back to St. Damian's and spent two hours in the out-patients' clinic. Then he went upstairs in the hospital. At five he came home. At six-thirty he had dinner in a restaurant on 86th Street. He then took in the newsreel at a movie, and came home to keep his office hours. I left Toomey on the job."

"Dr. Billig lives a full if not a rich life."

"I don't know why it ain't richer; he looks like a brainy character to me."

"Likely to get on in the world?"

"One way or another."

"Brains do not always mean worldly success, Indus," said Gamadge solemnly.

Indus replied as solemnly: "And crime does not pay; or so they tell us. Whatever he did, it hasn't paid him."

When he had gone there were stars out in the purplish vault of the sky. Gamadge went to his office, opened the filing cabinet, and got out the Crenshaw Shakespeare. He took it up to the library; and there, reclining on the cool linen of the chesterfield, read *The Tempest*. A certain passage made him smile:

> ...remember
> First to possess his books; for without them
> He's but a sot, as I am; nor hath not
> One spirit to command...Burn but his books...

Gamadge took out a pencil, underlined the last four words, altered *his* to *the*, then struck out *but* and the final *s*. *Burn the book*. Excellent advice indeed, books can be very dangerous. In fact, if this dark, ugly, dangerous case ever came to trial, it would be tried because of the Crenshaw Shakespeare.

CHAPTER TWELVE

The Jeremiah H. Wood

AT EIGHT O'CLOCK on the following morning—Friday, July the thirtieth—Gamadge received the report of Mr. Toomey. Toomey, looking for some reason somewhat amused, kept his eyes on his notebook. He was very official:

"The subject," he began, "finished with his evening batch of patients at a quarter to ten P.M."

"Were they in the humbler walks of life?"

Toomey raised his eyes.

"As Indus would say," explained Gamadge.

"They was. When the last one left, the doc got into his car, which he keeps parked outside the flat, and drove to Park. It's a westbound street, so that's where he had to go first. But he drove right back again to Lexington, and down town. I had a cab waiting from nine-thirty on."

"That's right."

"We drove down to the sixties, parked at a corner, and stood around a minute. Then the subject walked up the block to a private house occupied by a Mr. Henry Gamadge."

"No!"

Toomey, gratified at the effect that he had made, went on: "He stopped, looked up at the front—which was all dark—"

"I was in the library reading. Can't say my flesh crept or anything."

"He crossed the street and stood looking. A cop came along, and subject went down into an area. Cop didn't see him—"

"Good."

"But saw me at the corner and gave me an ugly look. Wouldn't you know? Always get the innocent bystander, don't they?"

"Often," said Gamadge, who did not think that the lantern-jawed Mr. Toomey looked particularly innocent.

"Subject came out of the area, stood around some more, and then came back and got in his car and drove to Third. We went down Third, then east to an address in the upper Fifties. I'll give it to you. He got out of his car, went up the steps, rang, and was let in. I went up and had a look; two old brick houses joined together, one of 'em walled up to the second story. Evidently some kind of an institution. Afterwards I got Information on the telephone; it's called The Jeremiah H. Wood Home. I looked it up in the Red Book. It's a home for mental cases, alcoholics and drug addicts."

"Perhaps Dr. Billig has a patient there."

"If so he gives good service; he stayed an hour and seven minutes. He came out at 11:33, drove home, and put out his milk bottle. I thought we were through for the night, but there I sat in my window. An hour later he sneaked out again. He'd garaged the car, so he took a Third Avenue car; I nearly lost it. We came back here."

"You don't say!"

"And went through the same performance all over again, except that there wasn't any cop. We came home on a Lexington Avenue bus, and the performance was over for the night by thirty-four minutes past one. Perhaps you need a bodyguard."

"Not with you and Indus on the job."

Gamadge dismissed Toomey with praise, and called Dr. Hamish. "Red," he began, "there's some sort of a private hospital or nursing home called the Jeremiah H. Wood."

"Probably. I never heard of it."

"It's down in the East Fifties."

"There are some still in town; most of them have moved out now to the suburbs."

"It's for mental cases, alcoholics and drug addicts. Red, I've got to get in there."

"Easiest thing you know," began Hamish with some enthusiasm, but Gamadge cut him short:

"Billig has a patient there, I think. I've got to find out."

There was a pause. Then Hamish said: "Not so easy without giving yourself away. You don't want to?"

"Certainly I don't."

Another pause. Then Hamish said: "Perhaps we can work it. Be down at the hospital in half an hour?"

"Coming now."

Gamadge took a cab to the Vandiemen Hospital, a speckless and glassy building, only to be distinguished from an apartment house by the sign on its awning. Here Dr. Ethelred Hamish performed miracles of surgery, and here, in his private office, Gamadge found him; dressed in white for operating, with a sort of white turban on his head and a sheaf of typed papers in his hand. Near him stood a super-nurse, handsome as everyone in Hamish's entourage was always handsome.

Gamadge nodded to the super-nurse, and said: "Good morning, Miss Walkley."

"Good morning, Mr. Gamadge."

"And blessings," continued Gamadge, turning to Hamish, "on the old dead pan. A heart beats under that snowy stuffing, I always said so."

"But not for you, light-weight, not for you." He addressed the super-nurse without turning his head. "This all on Mrs. Mullins, Miss Walkley?"

"Yes, Doctor."

"All right."

She went away, with a backward smile for Gamadge which he returned with interest.

"Lovely creature," he said in a sentimental voice.

"Very good nurse. The Jeremiah H. Wood, they tell me, is a private foundation, started in the 'eighties by one J. H. Wood, a merchant, who left his whole fortune to it. Began with a resident physician, is now run by a supervising nurse. There are resident nurses, and doctors send patients there, usually as a temporary measure—when they don't know what the devil else to do with them, you know. I needn't say that snoopers are not welcome; patients and their friends wouldn't like it.

"Now here's my suggestion: you remember Mrs. Mullins?"

Gamadge thought a minute. "The Hamish cook!"

"You ought to remember her; many's the wedge of cake she slipped us."

"And not a word out of her when she found we'd helped ourselves to something."

"Well, she's retired, and we thought she was comfortably settled with her married son and his family. But she's getting senile, and the daughter-in-law complains that she breaks dishes and annoys the children; obvious that they don't want her, and she can't be happy. I'm looking for some other place, not too expensive. I'd fork out the difference. Now of course this Jeremiah H. Wood place wouldn't do for her—"

"But I could go there and say I was looking around in behalf of Mrs. Mullins."

"That's right. And the best of it is that you could use my name; unless you mean to bust the place up?"

"Not at all."

"You may hear some manic-depressive complaining, and think something's wrong."

"I'll give the Jeremiah H. Wood the benefit of the doubt."

"I don't want to get mixed up in a mare's nest."

"Some day I must come up and give you a short frank talk on the use of the metaphor; but meanwhile I may be able to do you a favor you'll better appreciate. I know of a place that may really suit Mrs. Mullins."

"You *do*?"

"Upstate; nice old lady and her daughter, nice little farm. They've just buried their paying guest, and they wrote me for another to pay taxes with. They're used to taking care of old people. They have airtight stoves, they don't open too many windows on the aged, and they tell me they have a whole shed of firewood. Mrs. Mullins need never see her daughter-in-law or her brats of grandchildren again."

Hamish said eagerly: "I hope you'll write and get details for me. Fix the thing up. These cases are the hardest in the world to deal with—old age is so damned incurable." He handed the typed pages to Gamadge. "Here's Mrs. Mullins' file. And if you think anything is wrong at the J. H. Wood, or they won't let you in, I'll drop down myself."

"You're as good as you are beautiful."

Gamadge hastily departed, to take a bus down Lexington Avenue. When he had left it, and walked east, he found himself in a district with which as a pedestrian he was not familiar; he found it odd and gray. Streets were suddenly transformed into the ramp which carries passenger traffic to and from the Queensborough Bridge; that traffic being westbound only between the hours of five and eleven A.M.

Certain blocks to the east and south of this neighborhood, built up in a transition period, have the bleak look of decayed gentility. Not one dwelling is unconverted, and many of the flats have frankly turned into tenements; there are some of those oldfashioned apartment houses where dressmakers used to fit their customers in an occupational atmosphere of must, there are small shops in the basements, children scream and play in the empty streets.

The Jeremiah H. Wood, of brick with a brownstone trim, was unutterably dingy. Half of it had retained its high stoop and vestibule, the other half had had its basement windows sealed with brick; its blinds were all pulled down against the morning sun, it might have been closed up and deserted. Gamadge mounted the flaking steps and rang the bell.

A leaf of the front door was almost instantly flung open, and a little woman in an oldfashioned silk dress stood smiling brightly up at him. He said: "May I speak to the supervisor?"

"I am the supervisor. Come right in."

A very tall, big woman in crumpled linen came striding down the hall. She possessed herself of the doorknob, saying: "All right, Miss Gentry."

Miss Gentry turned and scuttled away into a room on the right. The big woman turned her sallow face and murky eyes on Gamadge. She asked: "What is it?"

"I wanted to see the supervisor."

"I am the supervisor."

Gamadge felt a little as he had felt as a boy at the waxworks. Which was the real ticket-taker, the real policeman, the real lady-tourist in the Alpine hat and eyeglasses? Which gloved hand would return his handshake if he dared one? He could still dream of those questionable shapes.

"The other lady is a patient?" he asked, coming into the hall.

"That Miss Gentry!" The supervisor shut the door. "We're short-handed, of course, and she pops out the minute the doorbell rings."

"No danger that she'll—er—pop off? Run away?"

"Oh, no. She never goes out. She's afraid of the streets. What can I do for you?"

"I was talking to Dr. Hamish at the Vandiemen Hospital about placing an old lady in a Home. My name's Gamadge. I thought you might be able to tell me whether the Jeremiah H. Wood—"

"Dr. Ethelred Hamish sent you here?"

"Oh, no; I was talking to him about the patient—she's all right, just getting a little weak in the head—and I had a list. It would be convenient here for her, but there's the question of expense."

"Don't get it in your head that we're cheap." She led the way into what seemed to be her office, a large room, once a library, with Jeremiah H. Wood himself, fully labelled and whiskered, over the mantelpiece. "I'm Mrs. Lubic," she said. "Have a chair."

She sat in a chair behind a desk, and Gamadge took another. The light that came through the brown shades was sickly; he could barely make out her strongly defined features, graying hair, heavy chin. She was looking at him curiously.

"It would be temporary," said Gamadge. "I'm more or less responsible—have assumed the responsibility for her comfort. We thought you might show me what you have vacant just now."

"Glad to."

Gamadge looked around him. "Interesting old place. Why did Jeremiah H. Wood found it, do you know?"

"He lived in this house we're in, and his son lived in the other. The son went under; drugs, alcohol, I don't know which. The family doctor said he could cure him at home, and did; so J. H. Wood made a will leaving both houses to be converted into a Home, and giving the doctor life-tenancy of the job. Out of gratitude, you know. When the doctor died there was a trust set up. We have only visiting doctors now; they visit their own patients. This patient you want to send here would have to engage one of our nurses to look out for her if she needs care; and if we have a nurse," added Mrs. Lubic, with a sardonic look.

"It sounds a little expensive. Did Jeremiah H. Wood's son

approve of this disposal of his father's property? Rather a grim reminder for him, I should say."

"Oh; by that time he didn't care; he died."

"Died?"

Mrs. Lubic's eyes glinted with a cynical kind of amusement. "Killed himself. I suppose after he was cured he didn't think life was worth living."

"It must be very bad to have a thing get its teeth into you like that."

Mrs. Lubic raised a heavy eyebrow. "We're so used to them here that we get a little hardboiled about them. And so do the relatives, believe *me*! We don't get many straight mental cases like Miss Gentry nowadays; they're sent out of the city. She's here because there isn't much of anybody left to move her; and she wouldn't like to go. She likes it. Has the run of the place. Well, shall we take a look?"

They went first downstairs to the basement of the other house, which ran straight from the bricked-up front windows to a shadeless yard. The adjoining yard was a drying ground.

"This is supposed to be a game room," said Mrs. Lubic, casting an uninterested glance at a decrepit ping-pong table, "but only the nurses use it nowadays. The trouble is," she went on, tramping out to the yard with Gamadge behind, "the least noise we make, somebody sends a policeman. The neighbors can play radios all night, and their children can scream and yell in the street under our windows, but just one yip out of us and there's a complaint."

"It must be pretty difficult, running a sanitarium in town."

"Well, most of our patients are in their rooms, in bed. When they're able to get up," said Mrs. Lubic in her hoarse voice, "they go elsewhere or they go home. The reason they come to us now is that there's no publicity. Nobody knows a thing. They get over whatever it is, and go home, and then after a while they come back. We *don't* tell!"

"Come back?"

"What do you think? Of course there are exceptions. Let's go upstairs before we get a sunstroke."

Gamadge saw a large dining-room on the first floor, which Mrs. Lubic said was never patronized by the patients; naturally not, since to be a patient at the Jeremiah H. Wood was to require privacy. The nurses had their meals there.

"Good for board-meetings, too, I suppose," offered Gamadge, but Mrs. Lubic shook her head:

"We don't have them any more. All that is done in some office downtown, thank goodness. Across here is our little surgery. Nice, isn't it?"

Gamadge admired the surgery, and then followed Mrs. Lubic upstairs and on a long tour of both houses; they were connected on every floor by double doorways cut through the walls. He saw a good many closed doors, several large and well-equipped empty bedrooms, one or two smaller ones, and a very small one with a skylight, on the top floor, which the supervisor said Mrs. Mullins could have reasonably cheap. It was very hot, had no bath, and was not what Gamadge considered cheap at all.

"You do get prices here," he murmured in a tone of admiration.

"Why shouldn't we? Jeremiah H. Wood Homes don't grow on every bush."

"I'm afraid this wouldn't quite do for poor Mrs. Mullins, aside from the cost."

"It comes in useful sometimes," said Mrs. Lubic carelessly.

They were halfway down the parlor flight of stairs when Gamadge, a step or so behind his guide, asked casually: "How is Dr. Billig's patient getting along?"

CHAPTER THIRTEEN

Take Me Home

MRS. LUBIC PAUSED a moment, strong fingers on the stair rail; then she resumed her ponderous descent to the lower hall. "We never discuss patients," she said.

"Perhaps Hamish will be able to tell me."

Mrs. Lubic reached the bottom of the stairs, turned, and looked at Gamadge; he was leaning easily against the newel post. She said: "Patients have privileges."

"And so do doctors. Isn't it staggering, sometimes, Mrs. Lubic," asked Gamadge with a smile, "to think what privileges they have, and what an amount of faith we must put in them?"

Mrs. Lubic said rather roughly: "We have to."

"And if a doctor *should* be a bad one—it does happen— what couldn't he get away with? But you must realize that, even more fully than a layman can."

Not once, during their entire tour of inspection, had Gamadge heard a sound or a human voice; but Mrs. Lubic glanced about her. Then she asked, staring at Gamadge:

"What are you talking about?"

"I couldn't do more than give you a hypothesis."

"Well, don't give it to me here. Come inside."

She walked into the office, waited for Gamadge, closed the big walnut door, and faced him. "Now what is this?"

"Let's sit down."

She sat on the edge of the nearest chair, without removing her eyes from his. He resumed his earlier seat. "Imagine this, Mrs. Lubic," he said. "A patient with no friends, or none available. He's in a strange apartment, sick. He calls in a strange doctor. The doctor tells him he's dying—let's say of leukemia. Gives him a drug—a sulfa drug, say—and gets him into the state a leukemia patient might be in. Tells him at last that he must go to a hospital, and drives away with him in a cab.

"But he doesn't take him to a regular hospital. He takes him to a nursing home—like this one."

A dark flush had begun to rise in Mrs. Lubic's sallow face. She remained silent.

"Where there are no resident physicians," continued Gamadge, "and where they take a doctor on trust; where they're a little hardboiled about these drug addicts. For of course by this time there is a narcotic drug in use—of course; and the patient is quietly drugged out of existence. Who gives the death certificate—collapse from drug addiction? Why, the doctor, of course.

"That day another patient, who really has acute leukemia, is taken to a regular hospital by our doctor, in another cab. He's entered there under the first fellow's name, of course; dies under the other fellow's name, and is buried under it in the other fellow's graveyard. The only catch is that a friend does turn up, and sees the body at the undertaker's. Well, this is only a hypothesis; did the friend see what the friend expected to see? Would the game ever have been played if there hadn't been a leukemia patient who looked like the other man?"

Mrs. Lubic said in her gruff voice: "Don't ask me questions. I'll ask you one. Why?"

"Well, that's not such an easy one. The financial motive doesn't emerge, unless it's connected with the victim's will. He'd made a will, it involved a hundred and fifty thousand dollars at least. If he died before he had a chance to change it—"

Mrs. Lubic said dangerously: "You couldn't talk to everybody like this, Mr. Gamadge; you might be sued for libel."

"Slander. I'm not talking to everybody, Mrs. Lubic," said Gamadge. "I'm talking to you, and you impress me as being one of the most intelligent women I ever met in my life."

Mrs. Lubic sat back in her chair, and looked at Gamadge in a fury of concentration. She said at last: "You're a detective. There is no Mrs. Mullins."

"Here's her file."

She made no move to take it. "I might call Dr. Hamish."

"But you won't."

Her fingers tapped the arms of her chair. "You're counting on the effect of any kind of an investigation on a place like this. Any talk—not scandal, just talk—and the patients run for it; and their doctors won't send 'em back. You're banking on that. Well, let's settle it. If you think one of our patients is somebody else, come right up and meet the party." She shoved herself to her feet. "I'd rather lose Dr. Billig's custom than the whole business." As Gamadge rose, she went on: "Now how will we fix it so you can be sure you're being taken to the right room?"

"Mrs. Lubic, I trust you implicitly."

"You do, do you?"

"If you hadn't a clear conscience I should never have got upstairs at all without a warrant."

Mrs. Lubic laughed hoarsely. "You're dead right. When my husband died he left me poor, and I had to do police work before I got my nurse's training. I used to be sent to look at joints before they raided them, and when the joint was wrong I never got any further than the front door. The trouble is I can't send for the nurse, because we don't leave the patient alone."

She tramped ahead of Gamadge, out of the office and up three flights of stairs. When they had again reached the top floor she halted.

"You wait here a minute till I get rid of the nurse," she said. "I don't want any gossip in the house. I'll send her out on an errand; they're always glad to go. Makes a change for them."

"The patient *can* be left, then?"

"It won't be half a minute."

She went through into the next house, and returned almost immediately. "O.K. You're an electrician."

"In name only, I hope?"

"Inspector."

They entered the hall that Gamadge had visited before, and Mrs. Lubic opened a door at the end of it. He walked past her into a pleasant room that overlooked the yard; green outside shutters were partly closed, mitigating the glare, and it was only after a moment that Gamadge made out the strong bars in the windows. An open door gave him a glimpse of the white tiles of a neat bathroom.

A woman of fifty or more sat between the windows, shuffling a pack of cards. Her hair was dyed a harsh shade of red, and her face—a large-boned, well-modeled face—was reddened as if by a permanent skin-affection and deeply lined. It looked slightly out of focus; all the features seemed blurred.

She was perfectly groomed; her long hands were white, her nails polished, her feet shod in crocodile shoes that had cost money. Her dress was not new—it was of pure silk, which dated it—but it was a long-sleeved summer dress that looked like an importation. On one arm she carried a red handbag.

"Man about the lights, Mrs. Dodson," said Mrs. Lubic. "Just a minute. He won't bother you."

Mrs. Dodson looked up, and her clouded eyes rested on Gamadge calmly. Then she put down her cards, rose to her feet, and supported herself by placing her hands flat on the table. She said in a muffled voice: "Get me out of here. Take me home."

Gamadge knew it well—the race, the type, the unmistakable clan to which Mrs. Dodson belonged; never, while she lived, could she lose its characteristics—that dominant, privileged, confident pose, that easy way with strangers, that driving will. He knew her background as if it lay unfolded before him— the ocean liners, the blue trains, the galas in European opera houses, the bridge dinners and benefit plays and concerts here in New York. But she had been out of her world a long time; that flaming hair was not her own taste.

Mrs. Lubic said in a practical, rather bantering voice: "Now, Mrs. Dodson."

Mrs. Dodson paid no attention to her. She kept her eyes on Gamadge, clasped her red handbag to her side, and repeated: "Take me home. I want to go home."

Mrs. Lubic shook her head at the patient. "You know that's no way to talk."

Gamadge, in spite of Hamish's warning, was unable to keep the old question out of his head: *Which is the real ticket man, the real policeman?*

He asked gently: "Where is it, Mrs. Dodson?"

"Where is it?" Her faded eyes searched his.

"Home, you know."

Mrs. Lubic asked in her hateful, bantering tone: "Yes, where is it? Go ahead and tell him, Mrs. Dodson. Go ahead."

Mrs. Dodson muttered something, glanced from side to side, stood irresolute, and at last gave way to discouragement. She sat down slowly, picked up her cards, and began to lay them out with the manner of one to whom cards have always been an important part of life.

Mrs. Lubic addressed Gamadge from a corner of her mouth: "Had enough?"

Gamadge nodded.

"Then wait for me downstairs. I can't go till the nurse gets back."

Gamadge went down, took a chair in the office, and sat smoking until Mrs. Lubic joined him.

He said: "I don't know whether I ought to be smoking."

She replied to this by taking a crumpled package of cigarettes out of the desk drawer, shaking her head at Gamadge's lighter, and scraping a match on its box. When her own cigarette was going, she asked "Well?" in a tone of grim amusement.

"I never was so depressed in my life."

"Glad of it. Serves you right for scaring the daylights out of me. That wasn't your party, I suppose?"

"No."

"She doesn't need any dope. She's dying on her feet of several things."

"Who on earth is she?"

"Just a drunk with a delusion. We don't know any more than that, it's none of our business. Old patient of Dr. Billig's. Some cheap hotel sent him an SOS last spring, and he paid the bill and got her here. She won't be with us long.

"I'll say this for her: she keeps herself up. Any other woman I ever saw would be in bed; but she's right in there pitching. Dyes her own hair, or tries to; goes through all the motions. Well brought up," said Mrs. Lubic, and took her cigarette out of her mouth to smile.

"Suicidal?"

"Just part of the mental collapse. She isn't depressed. Perhaps," and Mrs. Lubic, not smiling now, looked at her cigarette, "she thinks it might be a short cut home."

"No money?"

"A little annuity or something; it's enough to keep her here. Dr. Billig looks after it."

"Why does she hang on to her handbag like that?"

Mrs. Lubic glanced at him. "You don't miss much." She squinted through smoke. "There isn't a thing in it but junk, we looked when she first came. She might have had something lethal in it. Just junk, and change for a dollar. I suppose she remembers the time when she had a roll of bills with her all the time, and an extra diamond bracelet. She hangs on to the bag day and night, and sleeps with it under her pillow."

"Can she still endorse her checks?"

"What checks?"

"Her annuity checks."

"I don't know. Dr. Billig attends to that. Perhaps he has some authority, and guarantees she's alive. I don't know a thing."

Gamadge smoked in silence.

"Anyhow," said Mrs. Lubic, "you can forget that about the cab and the leukemia patient and—the undertaker's. Can't you?"

"Oh; yes."

"Just made it up to make me show you the patient? Dr. Billig will be pleased; of course I have to tell him."

"Of course."

"Is Dr. Hamish really in this?"

"Certainly not. Mrs. Mullins is his patient, that's all." Gamadge rose. "I'm greatly obliged to you, and I only hope you return my feelings of regard, Mrs. Lubic."

"I'm not as mad as I ought to be, if that's going to be a comfort to you." She eyed him with a curious look. "You're a funny one."

"Am I?"

"Are you a lawyer or something?"

"Not a lawyer. Something." Gamadge shook hands with Mrs. Lubic, whose grasp was flaccid; she sat sunken in her chair, gazing up as if for spiritual consolation at the portrait of the rather tragic J. H. Wood.

Gamadge went out into the baking street, and stood for a moment looking up at the grim frontage of the Home. He understood better now why such a paying proposition should be allowed to give a dingy first impression; *here*, it seemed to say, *you won't find front page news. Nobody of any importance to you comes here. We are beneath your notice.* Gamadge was quite certain that at least one inmate of the Jeremiah H. Wood Home would rate the front page; the inmate known as Mrs. Dodson.

He got into the first cab, and had himself driven to Dr. Billig's Lexington Avenue corner. Making sure that the doctor was not in sight, he walked quickly to the rooming house opposite the doctor's flat, and up a short flight of steps to the unswept vestibule. A card bearing the name *Toomey* was stuck in a frame beside a bell. He rang, the door clicked, and he plunged into an atmosphere of dusk and eld. He went up steep and narrow stairs, sagging and uncarpeted stairs whose treads were hollowed and whose banister shook under his hand, to confront Mr. Indus in the upper hall.

"I got you a nice place, Indus." Gamadge blinked upwards into darkness. "A cheerful, unusual place. Oldworld atmosphere and lots of privacy."

"It's the skylight being blacked out makes it so bad," said Indus. "Come this way."

They walked to the front of the house, and into a furnished room where a parlor suite of indigo velvet had been allowed through many summers to absorb dust and fade into gray. There was a studio couch, within which bedding was stuffed when not in use; the stuffing had been imperfectly done by Mr. Indus, who looked mortified and poked a no-colored corner of pillow-case out of sight. Then he joined Gamadge, who was considering whether to sit down on a hard chair.

"I wiped that one off," said Indus.

"Thanks." Gamadge sat on it. "Our friend seeing patients?"

"It's a minute early for them. He's home, though."

"I'm glad of that. I have a feeling that he won't keep office hours today."

"Why?" Indus leaned to one side of the open window, glancing across the street and down to the Billig office.

"He's had a telephone call. We're lucky to have caught him—he'll be shifting that patient of his from the J. H. Wood."

"Oh. Toomey said something. You found out there was a patient?"

"I saw the patient."

Indus regarded Gamadge with the faint smile of one who acknowledges the standing of a fellow-craftsman. "You did?"

"Just now. I'm going now to get a cab. When Billig comes out you can join me at the corner. We've got to keep after him."

"Find out where he takes the party?"

"Find out what she keeps in her handbag. I'm depending on that handbag—it may give us a clue to her identity. It's an old one; she paid a lot for it once—twenty dollars, perhaps—and she'd pay twice that now; she likes good old things better than cheap new ones."

"You think I can get a look at what she has in her handbag?"

"If you can't while she's on the move, I don't know how you ever can. It's our chance."

"Class, is she?"

"She's been down and out for some time."

"Will she go anywhere he says?"

"If he says he's taking her home."

"Home?"

"She wants to go home."

Indus considered this, looking at Gamadge. "Where?"

"I don't know that it exists any longer, even; but it was here in New York. She may not have seen it since the nineties. And for God's sake, Indus, don't call them gay."

"Weren't they gay?"

"Not particularly. Not for everybody. Not all the time."

"Looney, is she?"

"On that subject." Gamadge rose.

"Why does Billig risk moving her himself?"

"She's a very sick woman; if she collapsed he'd want to be on hand."

"You want me to get a squint at initials on the bag, or on a cigarette case or something?"

"Whatever there is."

"Wouldn't they remove identifying objects at that place— the J. H. Wood?"

"Why should they? Billig hasn't asked them to keep any secrets. They'd understand an alias, because she's a dipsomaniac; lots of people must go there under assumed names—but not criminals, so far as they know."

"Wouldn't *he* remove the objects?"

"I'm hoping he wouldn't notice them. He isn't the type to notice women's gadgets much."

"What'll you do if I don't find anything to identify her?"

"Do without. I don't absolutely need identification, Indus, but how I want it!"

Gamadge went down the blacked-out stairway and into the street. He hurried around the corner. The first cab that came by was driven by a tough citizen in an undershirt, who said he didn't mind a trailing job if there wasn't going to be any shooting.

"There won't be any." Gamadge handed him half a generous tip on account, promised him the other half when the trip was over, got in and waited. He did not have to wait long. Indus came, jumped into the cab, and said: "He's getting out his car. He's put a sign on his door—no patients this noon."

The cab never lost sight of the Billig car, and was separated from it only once by a changing light; but that separation was unfortunate, since it occurred just as Billig entered the block containing the Jeremiah H. Wood Home. The pursuers sat helpless while the doctor got out and rang, while Mrs. Lubic supported Mrs. Dodson out to the car and handed her dressing-bag in after her. The light changed again in time for them to follow the car to First Avenue, but Indus had now lost his first chance at the red handbag; the next chance would be his last.

CHAPTER FOURTEEN

Number 152593

Billig's car rounded the next block north, came back through 57th Street, and followed a stream of traffic up the ramp to the Queensborough Bridge. The cab shot after it just before the traffic policeman's hand rose against the oncoming tide.

"Friday, Friday, Friday," chanted the driver. "All going to Long Island, and what do we say when they ask us where we're going?"

Indus produced his license. "Crime business."

"Have we gas?" asked Gamadge, when the bridge was passed. The Billig car was going steadily on through blistering streets.

"Unless he's bound for Montauk," said the driver, who was getting up an interest in the pursuit.

Dr. Billig was not bound for Montauk; he turned off the highway, drove for twenty minutes, and at last drew up in a shady block, before a small stucco house. Children played in the neighboring yards, a bus went past the further end of the street.

The cab slowed, reversed, stopped short of the corner. Indus tore off his coat, wrenched the door open, and sprang to the ground. He dashed up the street; with his hat on the back of his head, the coat over his arm and the ends of his necktie flying, he was the very picture of a little man catching a bus. The cab driver and Gamadge watched him from the concealing angle of a board fence.

"What's he going to do?" asked the driver.

"I don't know."

Billig had got out of the car, and was with some difficulty persuading Mrs. Dodson to get out too. Her bag was in his left hand, and his right firmly grasped her arm. A small woman in a gingham dress was coming down the walk from the house.

Mrs. Dodson reached the sidewalk; there was a straw toque on her flaming hair, and she had the red handbag over her left arm. She was hanging back and shaking her head; this was not home, this was by no means home. The small woman had arrived, a smile on her round face, and was beginning to add her persuasions to the doctor's, when Indus plunged into the group. His right arm engaged with Mrs. Dodson's left, and swung her half way round; her handbag, stripped from her wrist, lay on the ground. It may not have fallen open en route; but when Indus, stammering apologies, arrested in full flight, began to scrabble at it, it *was* open, and had discharged its contents upon the grass border of the sidewalk.

The whole thing took no more than a few seconds, during which Mrs. Dodson stood bewildered, and Dr. Billig, both hands occupied, gazed down at Indus with rising annoyance. No more than that—Indus was too inept a figure to do more than annoy anyone. He pushed money and small articles back into the bag, pushed the bag into Mrs. Dodson's hand, and stood breathing heavily and excusing himself.

Billig took the bag, glanced within, and then dismissed Indus with a kind of sweeping motion of the arm that consigned him to his bus or elsewhere. Indus turned and ran on, to catch the next bus going east.

The watchers did not linger to see Mrs. Dodson's induction into the stucco house. They climbed hurriedly into the cab, and drove by way of the next intersecting street to the bus line. They pursued Indus' bus for several blocks. When it stopped, and Indus joined them, nobody said anything until the cab was on its way back to the bridge at the highest rate of speed by ordinance allowed.

Then Gamadge asked with some awe: "How did you think that up?"

"That's an old one. That's the way they get the women's handbags, and the only way they can get them, without tearing the lady's arm off."

"I thought *I* was pretty damn ruthless in a good cause, but really. Did you frighten the poor soul?"

"Frighten her? No. I don't frighten anybody."

The driver remarked: "That was some wad you stuffed back into that handbag. Or did you stuff it all back? And do I get a cut?"

"I was only looking for identifying papers," said Indus. "Those were big bills; hundreds."

"Could there have been two thousand dollars there, Indus?" Gamadge was sitting forward, braced by one hand on the window sill, his face and body turned towards his operative.

"Sure could."

"Get the identification?" asked the driver, idly.

"No," said Indus, his eyes on Gamadge's. Gamadge sank back into his corner and lighted a cigarette.

"No ration cards, even?" the driver was surprised.

"No. The lady might as well be living some other time," said Indus.

The cab was paid off, and the driver given the other half of his tip, near the Gamadge corner. Indus preserved an obstinate silence until they were in the house, a late lunch had been ordered, and he and Gamadge were alone in the library. Then, gazing steadily into Gamadge's face, he put his fingers into his right-hand trouser pocket and withdrew them holding a small object. He kept it palmed.

"Besides that wad of bills," he said, "there was only the usual junk that the women carry around with them. A handkerchief, a lipstick, a little flat box for rouge and powder, a pack of cigarettes, some small change, and—er—old stuff she's been toting around half her life and didn't even know she had. Like we do. You turn out all your pockets and you'll find this and that; you never use the things, but you wouldn't throw them away. And the women's pockets are their handbags.

"And when they get new handbags, they transfer the junk."

Gamadge asked: "Such as?"

Indus opened his hand. Lying on it was an oblong of metal with a hole in one end of it for a key chain. It was punched with a series of numbers. "Know what that is?"

Gamadge, staring at it, shook his head.

"That's a charge coin, an old charge coin. You got a coin like that, and you didn't have to wait for your package; they charged it to you when they saw your coin."

"They?"

"Stengel's. That's an old Stengel coin. Number 152593. It could be fifty years old. They used them until just a few years ago; then they changed to name plates, like the other stores— your name and address punched on. But these old coins had nothing but your number, and they had the name and address in their files. Have, I mean."

Gamadge looked from the coin to Indus. "That does it."

"But you want to keep the cops out of it, and Stengel won't give that name and address to you or me," said Indus. "Don't think they will!"

"I don't care." Gamadge took the Stengel coin in his fingers. "Of course she would keep this."

"Keep it? No woman thinks a store is going to close up an account on her. Hers may have been closed up long ago, but catch her throwing that thing away."

"I think you must be right." Gamadge put the coin in his wallet. "I think you must always be right, Indus."

"Only I don't know what the racket is. Billig's racket. I suppose you could put a woman away in a place like the J. H. Wood, get hold of her money? Only he left her a considerable roll, enough to buy herself out of most places."

"That's his roll. That handbag is his cache; and what a cache! They'd already searched it; they wouldn't bother with it again at the J. H. Wood. If you'd been a second longer returning it, Dr. Billig would have had you out cold on the pavement. He's a strong man; that bulk of his isn't all fat."

The telephone rang, and Gamadge answered it: "Schenck?"

"None other than he, and things are breaking."

"What's happened?"

Schenck never began with a climax, or allowed anything to impair his narrative style. He said: "We had the funeral."

"What was it like?"

"Short. The village turned out, and the step-niece of the late Crenshaw turned up in good time. She stayed all morning at the Stonehill House, and she's aroused a great deal of interest. What with her, and the crowd, Boucher and I had good cover. It's a big old cemetery, had to be enlarged several times since the first incumbents were tomahawked. Now it stretches right out to the edge of the mountain on the north, and they've built a stone wall around the whole thing for fear of landslides.

"I took in the proceedings from the east wall; Boucher parked the car on the road at the northwest corner, and sat slumped down. Did I mention that the bags would be in the car, packed and ready, in case we had to move?"

"I think you did."

"And the landlady paid for the day in advance? Mrs. Much. She wished we knew just how long we *could* stay; nothing she likes better than single gentlemen who don't know enough to complain about the beds and the coffee.

"There's an intersecting dirt road running along the west wall of the burying ground; Pike had his old car on that, and he came and stood at the graveside; he and Miss Daker were chief mourners, faced each other across the grave. Ceremony over at 2:15. Miss Daker had looked at Pike two or three times, seemed interested; he didn't pay any attention to her. He was dressed up in his store clothes, felt hat; looked less like a farmer and more like a commission agent. After the ceremony she went around and spoke to him, and he tipped the felt hat; very cool and stand-offish, no time for Miss Daker.

"But she went on talking, and finally they walked off to the gate in the west wall, and through it, and sat down on the running board of his car. The crowd was leaving, and I began to worry a little about Pike noticing Boucher. Not at all; he never glanced that way. I had to get down off my perch, of course, and stroll off a little way with some natives. They were full of Crenshaw's sad death from leukemia, and Mrs. Crenshaw not knowing anything about his being sick until he was dead, and her not coming to the funeral, and Miss Daker showing up to represent the family. It seems people had been asking Miss Daker a lot of questions, and she came through with some of the answers. She's a pretty girl, isn't she?"

"Very attractive."

"Nice little hat; the folks don't think it's very funereal, but they forgive her because she had a sudden trip from California and then this night trip to Stonehill. She's taking the hotel bus down to Unionboro; it catches the long-distance bus to New

York." Schenck added: "Gets in late. I hope she has somebody to meet her."

"She'll have somebody."

"Well, I kept an eye on the two sitting on the running board. They talked for ten minutes, and then they got up. Pike tipped his hat again, and she came along around the corner of the wall and up the road towards my group. Pike got into his car, and drove right over the edge of the mountain and off."

"Off?"

'That road he was on goes down into the next valley and to a little town on a branch railroad called Baylies."

"You mean he left for good?"

"Just like that, and Boucher after him. We don't know the country; Pike might have had a chance to take some side lane, and we couldn't risk that, naturally. Boucher just streaked after him, taking our bags.

"Our arrangement was that in case of a sudden breakup the one left in Stonehill would check out and go down to Unionboro. There's a good hotel there opposite the station, the Long Valley Inn. I'm taking the bus Miss Daker's taking. Goes at three-thirty. Now, don't get it into your head that Pike was making a getaway. In a sense he probably is, but he isn't running away from us. He drove off like anybody. He quit because he was ready to, that's all. Let's hope Boucher won't lose him."

"Let's hope."

"They'll have to stop for gas sometime, and Boucher will telephone me at the Long Valley Inn. I've got five minutes to send a note to Mrs. Much—tell her we're called away. From now on it's going to be tough, Gamadge, and it's Friday, and we have to be back on our jobs early Monday morning."

"I'm coming up."

"You *are*?"

"Tonight, if I can get a berth on the 12:01. At 8:52 tomorrow morning I ought to be with you in Unionboro."

Schenck was relieved. "I'll be glad to see you. If Boucher should send me a hurry call after midnight I'll leave a note for you here."

Gamadge, muttering that he hoped that wouldn't happen, went back to Indus. "I've got to beat it down to the Grand Central and try to get a reservation; I'm leaving town for a few days. Tell Toomey. You mustn't lose Billig, whatever happens. I've left plenty of cash with Geegan; you and Toomey had better have plenty on you, in case the doctor should leave New York. I don't believe he will."

"He's had time to get started already."

"I don't think he'll go."

"Has to watch that case in Queens? Even if it penetrates his mind that I might not have been running for a bus after all?"

"Even so."

Indus hurried off, looking worried. Gamadge went down to his office, wrote a letter, sealed and stamped it; then he got some papers out of his desk, put his hat on and went out. He posted the letter at the corner, and took the subway to the Grand Central. Then he went down town to keep appointments in his other office, the cubbyhole that overlooked Bowling Green.

When he came home it was nearly dinnertime.

"I got a berth on the night train to Unionboro," he told Theodore. "At least I got one on the car that finally gets to Unionboro. We shall put in hours at Springfield. Won't that be fun?"

"What hours?" asked Theodore.

"Four-thirteen till seven A.M."

Theodore was amused, but he turned grave: "You goin' to let Mrs. Gamadge know you're goin' away on a case?"

"I telephoned her that I was joining Mr. Schenck for the week end, and that's what I am doing. I have to go down town again after dinner, but I'll come back here to pick up my bag; please pack the small one for me."

"All those funny people been comin' in the house—young person wouldn't give her business, police and a burglar, those two men; and long distance from Mr. Schenck every five minutes: it's a case."

"Everything's a case nowadays, Theodore; I'm on cases all day and every day."

"That's different, that's the war. We don't mind those cases. We mind your old kind, and Mr. Schenck's kind."

"Don't tell her a word, Theodore."

Gamadge went back down town to the little office with the view of Bowling Green, to which a night watchman took him in the elevator. At half past ten the night watchman brought him down again and let him out of the silent building into the silent street. He was used to lower Manhattan at night, but this time he was not sorry to leave its great bastions for the comparatively animated subway. Even this, however, seemed lifeless; his train was a long time coming.

And when he changed to his local at 42nd Street, where there was something of a crowd, he found himself keeping clear of the crowd, away from the edge of the platform, when the local came in. He didn't think that tonight he would like the feel of being shoved.

At his own dark corner somebody asked him for a light; it was Toomey, cigarette in hand and hat pulled down.

Gamadge said: "Don't tell me our friend's back again."

"If you look along the block you'll see a piece of shadow that ain't a stone post."

Gamadge looked. Then he said: "I'm coming right out again with my bag. Stick around."

"Want me to walk along?"

"No, thanks; just stay here under the light. That'll do."

The hunched shadow lost itself among other shadows as Gamadge approached his steps. Gamadge let himself in, took his bag and a light topcoat from Theodore, and spoke to the cat

Martin. Then he came out again, walked to the corner, ignored Toomey, and hailed a cab. He thought of all the people who were now scattered about the country; of Mrs. Dodson in the little house in Queens, of Billig, Schenck, Boucher, all on the move. Of himself setting out reluctantly on this journey. All because Idelia Fisher lay in some mortuary, unconcerned.

CHAPTER FIFTEEN

Junction

GAMADGE HATED UPPER BERTHS only a trifle worse than he hated lower ones; he never really slept in them. Tonight he lay in his accustomed half-stupor when a tremendous jolt and shudder woke him fully—they were in Springfield.

He waited until more jerks and shuntings ended in the peculiar dead quiet of a train at rest. The car was in its siding until seven o'clock, when it would be picked up and taken on to Unionboro. He turned over and went to sleep.

A hard, persistent poking, aimed with expert precision at his shoulder, woke him again—the indescribably relentless poke of a porter's knuckles through the curtain of a sleeping berth. He looked out.

"You Mr. Gamadge?"

"Yes."

"Certainly am glad. Folks don't like to be woke up. Telegram for you, sir." The porter's face showed respect, a certain awe: "Urgent. Federal business, sir."

Gamadge took the yellow envelope, looked at the porter, and opened it. He read:

HENRY GAMADGE ON BOARD CAR 70 NEW YORK TO
UNIONBORO SPRINGFIELD STATION SPRINGFIELD
GET OFF SPRINGFIELD WILL JOIN YOU WITH CAR
ABOUT EIGHT THIRTY JUST HEARD FROM BOUCHER
SCHENCK

Gamadge looked at his watch. It was twenty minutes to seven; he said: "Can do."

"Yes, sir. I'll let down the steps."

Gamadge had no time to wash. His impressions of Springfield Station and of Springfield itself were vague, remained vague even when he had had a cup of coffee in an early restaurant. Then he found an early barbershop and had the works—shampoo and shave, hair cut and facial massage—and began to shake off the effects of his short and troubled night. By the time he came back to the station it was half past eight o'clock; Schenck did not arrive, and Gamadge sat in the morning air, on the station platform, until half past nine.

Schenck drove up, neat and business-like as usual, but there was a dimness on his lustre. He opened the car door: "Sorry to be late."

"I've been inquiring for more telegrams." Gamadge climbed in.

"No time for that." Schenck turned the car and drove southward as though he knew where he was going very well. But he said nothing more, and after a minute Gamadge asked: "Well, what's the trouble?"

"We think Pike's vanished."

Gamadge sat mutely looking at Schenck's profile.

"I know. Say it, say it. But how do you think we feel," asked Schenck, "after doing all the work?"

"Do you really think I'd blame you?"

"No, but it's sickening."

"Are we—excuse me for asking—are we going back to New York?" asked Gamadge mildly.

"No, just out of town to this little place—golf club—the Crab Apple Inn. It's an old mansion done over, and it's very shick. Shicker," said Schenck, "than the big places on the river. Only they've lost their custom for just now. Boucher's there; or at least he's sitting on a knoll on the golf course."

"Is he?"

"It was on the cards we might lose Pike," said Schenck violently, "but not like this. All we can think of is that there was a car waiting to pick him up, and Boucher says that's almost impossible. You don't know what Boucher's been through. Poor little guy's about used up."

"I'm awfully sorry."

"That's all right, he's full of beans yet. Won't admit we've lost Pike, and I don't see how we can have. But I'll tell you the story. It *was* a getaway, all right."

"From you two?"

"No, no; that's out; you'll see why. But he deliberately lost himself. What happened was this:

"I told you how Boucher drove after him down the mountain. It was an old dirt road lined with trees; Boucher could see Pike's car a long way ahead, and Pike never looked round. When they got to this Baylies Pike was already in the one and only garage; selling his car."

"Very wise of him."

"That's when Boucher knew for a fact that Pike was going to disappear if he could. Boucher drove right over to the railroad station, parked behind the bushes in the weedy lot beside the tracks—you know those lots—and asked when the next down train was due. It was due in an hour; Unionboro the first station, and then all stops to Boston via Springfield.

"The next up train wouldn't come along until seven at night.

"Boucher took his big chance right there, and his judgment was good; he got in the car again and drove straight for Unionboro, where he picked me up. We were there on the platform when the train from Baylies crawled in; if Pike hadn't been on it, of course we would have driven back to Baylies and tried to follow up from there. But Pike was on the train, and he got off.

"He was lugging a big heavy suitcase; been living in it for a long time, you know. He lugged it right across the square to the Long Valley Inn, and he registered: George Pike, Cumberland Avenue, Springfield, Mass. Only I don't think there is any Cumberland Avenue in Springfield. Boucher got a squint at the card; by that time, of course, I was the one Pike mustn't see.

'By this time Pike was (as I said) a respectable-looking small town guy, small agent or tradesman; the day clerk at the Long Valley didn't think much of him, but he gave him a room, no bath. He went up to it, lugging his own bag; and he didn't act like a man who cares much for lugging a bag, either.

"The Long Valley is one of those old coaching taverns, with lots of the original rooms and gadgets about it; quite a show place when there's any motoring trade. Now there isn't, and the place is pretty dead; too expensive for the local trade. There's another station hotel—The American House—looks terrible. Pike wasn't having any of that. In the money, we decided. And of course from then on we had to keep our eyes open, even if it did look as though he had settled down for the night.

"We parked the car in the garage behind the Inn, had it all ready to start with its nose pointing out, and made sure there was all-night attendance so that we could get at it early if we wanted to. Pretty ironical."

"Was it?"

"You'll see. Well, the Inn has a lot of its old fixings left, as I said, and one of 'em's a kind of a covered way that runs across from the living quarters to the kitchen wing, with a space under it for the coaches to drive through to the stables. Gate-house. When we drove in under it to the garage we both noticed it, and noticed that it had windows back and front; if you were up in it you could watch both entrances to the Inn; all the entrances to the Inn.

"It being his watch that night, we decided that he'd better watch from there. It's nothing but a passage; we took chairs there and sat and talked about the case until supper time. Boucher liked the idea that Pike might be going back to Stonehill."

"Did he?" Gamadge smiled.

"Liked it a lot; the idea of Pike hiding up there in the boarded-up Crenshaw house, nobody knowing it."

"Why hiding there?"

"Digging for Uncle Crenshaw's buried savings. I think they must bury more savings in France than they do here, or Boucher wouldn't have been so sold on the notion. The talk up in Stonehill was that old Uncle Crenshaw had only left enough in the bank to bury him, but that he probably had cash stowed away. But isn't that always the talk?"

"Did Boucher think that Pike had chanced on some indication of hidden money, and concealed the knowledge of it from Crenshaw?"

"He was fooling with the possibility."

"Pike had had a long time to find that buried treasure."

"Boucher thought it might be in the ground, and Pike was too dumb to read the plan, or map, or whatever he had. But Boucher wasn't entirely serious about it, you know; he was just taking it into consideration. You haven't given us much to go on in this case, Gamadge."

"I'll tell you all about it when we join Boucher."

"He was wrong, anyway. Pike had an early supper and went to bed; or I suppose he went to bed. Boucher and I had a later meal, and I went to bed. Boucher went back to the gate-house. He was to call me early; he did.

"At six o'clock I was knocked awake; message brought across the square by a boy. Here it is."

Schenck took a hand off the wheel and fished in a pocket. He brought out an envelope, scrawled in pencil:

> *We are leaving on the half past six bus Boston via Springfield. Get to bus stop in Springfield before we do if you can.*

"It seems," continued Schenck, "that Boucher hadn't a second to call me. It all happened in no time—Pike must have had his seat engaged on this bus, which starts from up state at God knows what hour in the morning, and gets to Springfield at 8:30 A.M. You can engage a seat on it through the Inn. Pike pulled a fast one that time; we never knew a thing about it—he never went outdoors from the time he came with his bag to the time—before six—when he walked out of the front door, lugging the bag as per usual. We knew about the other bus, of course, the one Miss Daker took for New York yesterday afternoon; I saw her get on it myself at four P.M. We never thought of this terrible thing that stops everywhere and ends up in Boston.

"Boucher of course left the Inn just as he was—luckily he had his hat, you can't separate Boucher from that snap-brim of his—and streaked after Pike. Bus came in, Pike's suitcase was stowed, and Pike told them Springfield; Boucher had just time to grab himself a seat—right in the rear—and scribble that note to me, and pay a boy to deliver it. And the way he did get a seat was to hold a kid in his lap. The mother was French Canadian, and they had a great talk all the way, Pike was not paying any more attention to them than he paid to the driver. I'll say this much for that Sunrise Special, it's quite easygoing and human. The Canadian woman and Boucher fixed it all up between them, Boucher giving the kid a quarter for itself and paying the extra fare."

"Boucher ought to have a medal."

"How about me? We now return to me, checking out from the Long Valley Inn, lots of time, I'd have no trouble passing the bus, all O.K. I wasted no time, though; threw our things into the bags, and walked out to the garage with the night clerk very kindly carrying one suitcase for me. We got to the garage, and found it locked up tight and not a soul there.

"The night man, old war emergency substituting for the one who's now in the Coast Guard, had gone home at his usual hour without waiting for the day man; locked up and took his key with him. The day man's wife was sick; we telephoned, but by that time he'd started from back country somewhere. The end of it was that I got my car and got going at 7:15. I didn't overtake the bus; I never even caught up with it."

"Naturally you didn't."

"But I found a note from Boucher waiting for me at the bus stop in Springfield; it said that he and Pike had changed buses, and that I was to come after them to a place called the Crab Apple Inn; the man at the bus stop gave Pike directions about a short cut from a filling station, but Boucher didn't know the route they'd follow; I had to get that myself.

"I got it and followed. Saw the short cut—a path through the woods that comes out on the golf course behind the Inn. I drove around by road; circling the woods north and then west. I stopped short of the Inn behind a screen of elms, but Boucher saw me—can see all the roads—from his lookout on the golf course; he came down and told me his awful story."

They were now driving along a pleasant highway, green fields on their left and right, wooded country ahead. In front of them loomed a blot on the scene which Gamadge recognized as a filling station. Schenck continued, his eyes on the road:

"Pike didn't see Boucher get off the bus; Boucher took care of that; but the trouble was that Pike had to be allowed to walk off, dragging his suitcase, into the woods by that footpath, and Boucher didn't dare even start after him for five minutes. Never saw or heard him once. When the trees began to thin, Boucher waited again; and when he came stealthily out on the golf course, there wasn't a soul in the landscape. Crab Apple Inn down in a hollow in front, caddie house near it on the right, big garage on the left, and the road I afterwards came by passing the Inn and getting lost in the distance.

"Pike had had ten minutes to vanish in, and he's gone; disparu. We think he had a car waiting by appointment, and simply got in and went off—anywhere you like to guess. Boston? No. He'd have arranged to go on by that first bus.

"Wooded roads, you know, car wouldn't be seen half a minute after it left. And Boucher had no car; and he hardly dared come down off the golf course. Because Pike just possibly *might* have checked in at that Crab Apple Inn, miracles do happen. He just might have joined the kitchen staff, or gone to the garage, or holed up in the caddie house—which is a one- or two-room bungalow, with a lean-to shed for the caddies. But why hide in a caddie house, when he wasn't hiding at all, and had every chance, even as early as that—nine o'clock—of meeting up with golfers or caddies or a caddie master?

"Well, of course Boucher had to make inquiries down at the Inn. He went carefully, along the edge of the trees, and tried first at the back door. Cook said nobody had come that way with or without a suitcase, no new man at all, and she wasn't lying. From there he cut across to the garage; not a soul in it, all open. Then he walked up to the front door of the Inn and very reluctantly entered the lounge. He wasn't feeling presentable, and no wonder. He's a neat little guy, but he was getting a trifle grubby."

Gamadge interrupted: "Has either of you had any breakfast?"

"Boucher had a cup of coffee while he was waiting for the second bus to get under way. I haven't."

"Words can't express how I feel about all this."

"It's losing Pike we care about now. A very nice woman runs the place; she was at her desk. She said nobody had checked in, no newcomer at all. *She* wasn't lying. No, she told him, his friend hadn't come.

"He went out again, and he thought it over; would he or wouldn't he try the caddie house? If Pike was there—and why should he be, where would he go *from* there?—what would happen if Boucher walked in on him? Boucher doesn't give a hang about himself—he's too old a hand for that, and to tell you the truth I don't think he thinks he has much to live for now—but it wouldn't do you much good if he was shot. However, he finally did edge up to the place. It's only a few yards from the side door of the Inn; convenient for the golfers. Door was shut; he peeked in. Nobody, not a sound. He went in; nothing. Two rooms and a washroom. Empty.

"He went back up to the first tee and sat down behind the knoll and leaned out to watch the road; and the Inn.

"That's where he was when I drove up; as I said. He came down and told me the story, and then went back up the hill while I drove in for you. There isn't a house within a mile of the Inn, and the place is as quiet as a tomb. No cars, no golfers. Here's where we turn."

They left the filling station on their right, and drove along the edge of the woods. Pastures rolled away to the south and east. Gamadge leaned out to look at the footpath along which Pike had lately walked; along which Boucher had not dared to follow him too closely.

"What Boucher and I want to know," continued Schenck, "is why Pike ever came to the place at all; unless to be picked up and go on somewhere else. And you'll notice he left a trail."

"Yes," said Gamadge with a smile, "Pike left a trail."

"The Crab Apple is marooned; you'd think a bus conductor would remember somebody asking about the Crab Apple and getting off at that filling station."

"You would."

"Pike doesn't seem to care whether he's followed or not."

"Why should he, if he can vanish?"

"He's miles away by now. Boucher feels pretty sick."

"I'm sorry he does."

They drove northward around a curve in the road. Here were elms, screening a fine old house with a fine old sloping lawn. Schenck slowed the car, stopped it; a small figure began to descend a green knoll in the middle distance, and approached them along the dark wall of trees that fringed the nearer side of the property.

Alexis Boucher, limping a little, came up to the car. He was thin and rather pale, with gray hair; he had a small gray moustache, a high Norman nose, and half-closed gray eyes. In his gray town "complet," his somewhat battered gray felt hat, his dusty black shoes, he could not have looked much less conspicuous if he had been not Pike's shadow but his own. When he spoke, gently and in a low voice, when his half-closed eyes rested on the person spoken to, that person knew very well without being told that M. Boucher had the authority of a long training and a vast experience.

He now laid a hand on the ledge of the car window. "Mr. Gamadge," he said, not in apology but in regret, "this is too bad."

"Boucher, for God's sake get in here and rest yourself."

Boucher got into the back of the car, sat down, and stretched out one leg. "Now that we have the car again—this splendid car, how well it followed our Pike to Baylies!—I don't feel so helpless. At least if he is still here, he won't get away."

"What do you think? Did he get away?"

"I don't know. He may very well have got off with friends while I was waiting till the coast was clear. He had ten minutes. But I cannot answer for what he is capable of. Mr. Gamadge, this Pike is formidable."

CHAPTER SIXTEEN

Disappearance of Pike

GAMADGE, his elbow on the back of the seat, had turned to face Boucher squarely. "Formidable, is he?"

"Even Mr. Schenck admits it now."

Schenck said: "I admitted it as soon as I heard about that round trip of his—from Stonehill to Unionboro via Baylies. There's more to him—" Schenck's mouth turned down at the corners—"than meets the eye."

"Now, literally!" agreed Boucher. "But I always thought so. The trouble was that I never saw him close, and—of course—I usually saw the back of his head. But I got one clear view of him at the funeral, one.

"And another trouble was and is that I don't know the American types. In France I should have known whether he really was a commission agent in a small way; petit bourgeois, or mechanic rising out of his milieu by the ambition to be earning a salary instead of wages. But here I could not tell. You in this country—so many of you, some most successful—came from a farm. So many like to—what is it?—*go back to the farm.*

In vacation. To relax, take off their collars, help to pitch the hay. They can speak like the men who pitch the hay for a living."

"And often do," said Gamadge gravely.

"Then what was Pike? A country type, as Mr. Crenshaw described him, or an equal of Crenshaw's socially—*in the world*—masquerading?"

"I dare say our values often do seem a little mixed to a European."

"No, you are yourselves. Your values are your own. But whatever the truth about Pike might be, I knew that he had an inner force. The force of the rustic philosopher, and innocent? Or the balance and the confidence of a man playing a part, playing it superbly? I thought that he was dangerous—because to me there was something wrong about him. Not spiritually, you know; physically. I can't explain this feeling. I couldn't study him. But there was something louche. Can you translate that for me?"

"Equivocal? It won't do—not strong enough."

"It will do. Equivocal. And that's all I can say."

"Well, that's quite enough. Now, since we can't even guess where he got to if he was met and carted off, let's go and register at the Crab Apple. You and Schenck must be fed and have a good rest, and I won't say no to a nap myself, later."

Boucher heaved a deep sigh and sank back against the upholstery. Schenck drove up to the Inn, straight past the front to the side door; a porch, constructed for carriages in the past, offered conveniences for unloading baggage—the door of the car just cleared it.

"If they're short-handed, like every other place we've been at in the last two days," explained Schenck, "we may have to carry our own bags."

No porter appeared. They got out, unloaded the bags, and went into a short side hall. Gamadge led the way through an arch into the big lounge on the right.

A stout lady with cropped gray hair, steel spectacles on her nose, came from behind her table-desk to greet them. She wore the roughest and toughest of Harris tweeds, her manner was easy, and her voice amiable but gruff.

"Rooms?" she asked, with a fleeting glance at Boucher.

"For a night or two."

"I'm the manager and proprietor. My name's Crabbe. Miss Crabbe."

"Mine's Henry Gamadge, and these are my friends Mr. Boucher and Mr. Schenck. We're all from New York," said Gamadge, "arrived by the Unionboro Express."

"At Springfield? It doesn't stop." Miss Crabbe looked benignly interested.

"We got off, but unfortunately our clubs didn't."

"What a shame. Anything can happen now."

"And it doesn't look well to bat an eye."

"No, golf clubs don't loom so very important nowadays."

"Except to owners on holiday. The thing is, Miss Crabbe, we've heard great things of the Crab Apple; we still hope very much that they can fix us up at the caddie house."

Miss Crabbe was sympathetic. "You know how things are," she said. "There's plenty of room for you, but you won't find the greens what they ought to be, and we only have a few caddies, and they're on call. Nobody gets here. Our caddie master is in the Air Force, and old McBride, who was once our pro, seldom shows up. But he doesn't live far away, and he used to make excellent clubs. He ought to be able to fix you up with spares, if you can get around with less than usual. I only carry five myself."

"I'll take you on with four," said Gamadge, "if McBride has a brassie."

Miss Crabbe was delighted. "But I'm not going to play a foursome with three men," she said. "Not any more. Just register, will you, and I'll call Arthur."

She gave them cards, and rang. Gamadge, signing, asked: "I wonder if Mr. Schenck and Mr. Boucher could have a breakfast lunch and a good long quiet afternoon? They've been on the go, and they won't want to play till tomorrow. I might have a tray of lunch in my room; I'm tired myself."

"Good idea. I'll have your friends' trays taken up."

A houseman appeared. Boucher followed him upstairs, looking as though he might not be able to reach the top landing.

"You have a fine house here, Miss Crabbe," continued Gamadge, his elbows on the counter. Schenck lingered beside him.

"Mine." Miss Crabbe put the cards away. "I wanted to go on living in it, so a lot of my friends helped me to turn it into an inn, and had the golf course laid out."

"Lovely place. Do you get many residents?"

"Not now. At present we have one young woman, who's been here before; golfer. Nobody to play with. And we have a couple for the week end."

"We're rather disappointed—I mean my friend Boucher was—not to find a friend of ours here."

"Oh; yes. I thought when you all came in that you were the friends he'd been inquiring for. I couldn't understand how you'd lost one another."

"We had business in Springfield, and Boucher decided not to wait for us in case we were detained. He came out in a cab, and then took a preliminary survey of the golf course. We *were* detained—very much so."

"Oh, I see. Poor Mr. Maxwell came by bus; dragged his bag through the woods! Couldn't get a cab for love or money."

"If Mr. Maxwell," said Gamadge, smiling, "is a tall, blond gentleman with a fair complexion, he's our Mr. Maxwell."

"For Heaven's sake," exclaimed Miss Crabbe, "how stupid I am! I might have known. The fact is that he came right in by the side door, though, and I didn't know he was here until Mr. Boucher had inquired and left. Mr. Maxwell went straight up to join Mrs. Maxwell. It's her first visit to the Crab Apple, but he was here before, you know—with that invalid friend of his, that nice Mr. Crenshaw."

Schenck's elbows slid along the counter, but he recovered himself.

"Poor Crenshaw, yes," said Gamadge.

"I was so sorry to hear from Mr. Maxwell that he died. They were here two weeks, June first to fifteenth…If Mr. Boucher had only mentioned Mrs. Maxwell—"

"We didn't know she was going to be here."

"Spoil your foursome, will she?" Miss Crabbe was amused. "She came up from New York last night; luckily *she* got a cab, arrived at nine."

"Don't tell them we're here; give her a day," laughed Gamadge. "We'll surprise them at dinner. We'll be more or less in eclipse till evening, and I assure you, Miss Crabbe, that the last thing we want to do is to talk to Mrs. Maxwell."

Miss Crabbe was indulgent to masculine preferences. "I won't say a word to either of them."

Gamadge took Schenck's arm and piloted him through the archway, out of the Inn, and along the flagged path to the caddie house. Schenck, walking as in a gentle stupor, said nothing until they had entered a large, woodsmelling room that combined the functions of office, lounge and caddie-master's domain. Behind it was a dressing-room, and to the right a workshop.

Schenck sat down on a bench. He asked dully: "Maxwell is Pike?"

"Of course. I was in great agony while we talked to Miss Crabbe—delightful woman, isn't she? But I counted on the theory that Mr. Maxwell would be tired and hot after carrying his bag through the woods, and would remain in conference with Mrs. Maxwell for some time. We must be very careful not to let him see us yet; that can't happen until I've made a telephone call and had a reply to a telegram."

"You didn't seem much surprised when we discovered that Pike had turned into a light-haired, light-complexioned golfer. Why did you describe him that way?"

"You really need to be told?"

"Yes," said Schenck, his eyes snapping angrily. "I do."

Gamadge came and sat down beside him. "Pike has been here before, as we learned from Miss Crabbe. He knew all about this caddie house. By the time Boucher came out of the woods, he was in there." He nodded towards the dressing room. "Washing off his sunburn and washing the brown rinse off his hair."

"You can't wash dye off under a water tap."

"Not dye—rinse. Mrs. Howard Crenshaw uses it; Lucette Daker told me so."

Schenck's eyes had an inward look. Presently he said: "When you described Pike as a blond you hadn't heard from Miss Crabbe that he'd been here before—under the name of Maxwell, and with Crenshaw."

"No, but I'd heard a lot about that ragged brown hair of Pike's, and that sunburn. Why ragged hair? Because he couldn't go to a barber's and have it cut? You yourself suggested 'home' cutting. Why sunburn? Sunburn is a disguise in itself; and sunburned skin has a shiny look about it; like grease paint, you know. And Pike had been described by Crenshaw as having a gallows complexion."

"By Crenshaw?"

"I'll explain later. The point is that Crenshaw probably used the phrase literally—as descriptive of the color a man is likely to be if he's on his way to be hanged. Shakespeare, from whom the phrase was quoted, or rather in whose play the phrase was marked, probably meant by 'complexion' the man's nature; the nature of the criminal—I'm convinced that when Crenshaw saw that phrase in *The Tempest* he thought of Pike—Pike as he really was under his disguise. A pale-skinned, light-haired man; but that's only my private notion."

"I might agree with you," said Schenck dryly, "if I knew what you were talking about."

"The immediate thing is to find evidence that Maxwell is Pike."

"We get that through Boucher and Miss Crabbe."

"We only know through them that Pike went into the woods with a suitcase and that Maxwell came into the inn with a suitcase."

"Pike was on the bus; Maxwell wasn't."

"You know how those things go. The theory might be that Boucher didn't see Maxwell. We want something definite. It won't help for Boucher to say that he thought Pike was louche, that's too theoretical. But we know why he thought Pike was louche; because the color of his hair didn't go with the color of his eyes—Boucher knows all about average types—and because Pike's manner wasn't right. It wasn't right for Boucher because it had that inner force; and Pike didn't seem to be a man whose inner force could spring from spiritual grandeur. Let's look at the workshop and the washroom."

In the washroom they found no more than a large collection of grubby paper towels; but in the workshop they found rags in a tin waste basket. Most of the rags were polishing rags of McBride's; some of them, unnoticeable among the others, were covered with reddish-brown grease and chestnut-brown stain.

"We'll leave them," said Gamadge. "Evidently they're not put in the incinerator every day."

"Smart of him not to put them down the drain," said Schenck. "If they stopped up the plumbing they'd be fished out and noticed. He rubbed the grease off on them, and finished the job with soap and water in the lavatory. But where did he get the time?"

"Boucher gives him ten minutes; let's say three to get into the caddie house, and seven to do the cleaning up. More; Boucher went to the back door of the Inn, to the garage, and around to the front to ask questions of Miss Crabbe. Five minutes more at least."

"He could wash in twelve or thirteen minutes, but he didn't have time to change into the other clothes he had in his bag. Shoes, too. No wonder that suitcase was heavy; he must have had a complete wardrobe of decent clothes in it."

"He didn't need to change his clothes. He couldn't risk not getting rid of the grease paint and the hair rinse—it wouldn't take much of that to color very light hair, by the way—but he was only going to dash from the caddie house across to the Inn and up to his room."

"To his wife. Maxwell has a wife; did you know *that*?" Schenck eyed Gamadge piercingly.

"Well, I thought he had something of the sort."

"Why?"

"We'd better go back to the Inn; you want your breakfast. I'll tell you in your room."

They found Boucher—whose room communicated with Schenck's by way of a bath—devouring his melon, bacon and eggs, toast and coffee. Schenck's tray arrived. While they ate, Gamadge sat on the deep ledge of the window, which overlooked the front lawn, and gave them a précis of the case. He began with Idelia's visit to him on the evening of the twenty-eighth, and omitted no detail except the contents of the letter which he had mailed the day before.

"There's just one thing," he confessed, "that I'm leaving to your imagination; and all it amounts to is an idea of mine. I shan't tell you about it until I've had a reply to a telegram that I must send today; because if it doesn't come off, then you won't be disappointed."

"You mean we won't find out where you went wrong," said Schenck.

Boucher poured his third cup of coffee. He listened and said nothing; but he was smiling.

"Perhaps I have gone wrong." Gamadge was quietly smoking, his eyes on the ancient turf and the ancient trees that had been Miss Crabbe's family's for a hundred years.

Schenck said: "Mrs. Maxwell is Mrs. Crenshaw. She never took the Century to Chicago at all; she came up here. She told Pike—Maxwell—about that brown rinse. It's a conspiracy, and you guessed it when you saw that note that Crenshaw made in the margin—*Cherchez la femme*. He knew that his wife and this fellow were up to something.

"You suspected her, so you never said a word to her about the underlined passages and the rubbed-out notes in the family Shakespeare.

"Billig was the third member of the gang. He got two thousand dollars for the job, but they may not know that he killed the Fisher girl; killed her as soon as he heard from you that she was making inquiries and stirring things up. And he went after you because he was afraid she'd told you something, and that *you* might upset the conspiracy.

"But what in the name of Pike *is* the conspiracy? Mrs. Howard Crenshaw and Pike and Billig didn't conspire to get rid of Crenshaw, because he died of leukemia. Didn't he?"

"He did."

"It wasn't for the purpose of preventing Crenshaw from changing his will; he could have managed that at Stonehill, or when he first got to the hospital. You made up that story at the Jeremiah H. Wood Home to scare Mrs. Lubic into letting you see the patient. Why did you want to see the patient—that Mrs. Dodson—though? I don't get that point at all. Who did you think she might be? You couldn't simply have had a hunch that Billig was hiding two thousand dollars in her handbag? There are no such hunches."

"None."

"And there doesn't seem to have been any insurance swindle. If there was insurance it'll come out later, but I don't see how there can be anything in that."

"Neither do I."

"As for that book, the busted Shakespeare, none of the parties concerned seems to care anything about it. They don't seem to have known that the Fisher girl had it, and if they did they haven't tried to get it away from her." He looked at Gamadge. "Why should they get it away from her? Because Crenshaw may or may not have been thinking of Pike when he underlined that part about the gallows complexion?"

"No."

"And *cherchez la femme* didn't mean anything to you until subsequent events made it mean Mrs. Crenshaw...I suppose she did come from California by plane when she says she did?"

"Yes."

"That's so, the girl was with her. The girl can testify that she didn't give a hang about her husband, but what of it? Are you going to invoke the Mann Act because Pike's week-ending with somebody else's widow? Count me out. At her age and in the circumstances that would be a little too tough," said Schenck, "even in Massachusetts."

"I shouldn't think of doing anything so vulgar as to invoke the Mann Act against the Maxwells," said Gamadge solemnly.

"Well then, what are you going to invoke? And how are you going to tie me in?"

"Just wait till I get a reply to one of my telegrams."

Boucher was smiling. "Prodigious," he murmured.

"You think so?" Gamadge looked gratified.

"And formidable."

Gamadge left his friends to their repose and went to his own room. It was on the northwest corner of the Inn, and it had a nice little balcony overlooking formal gardens; the houseman, caught as he was departing with the breakfast trays, explained that the Maxwells' suite was at the back of the house. Gamadge was pleased to know that he could take the air in the course of the afternoon. He unpacked his bag, and then furtively descended to the telephone booth under the front stairs.

He called Western Union and dictated three telegrams; none of them contained any more than the address and the telephone number of the Crab Apple Inn. One of them went to Geegan, one to Theodore.

CHAPTER SEVENTEEN

'Arts

GAMADGE WAS LOOKING forward to a shower before lunch. He had got so far as to remove his coat and tie when the fancy took him to step out on his little balcony and have a cigarette there. He was leaning on the rail, enjoying a prospect of flowerbeds in bloom, when he was startled by a voice that sounded almost in his ear. It said in friendly but unmusical accents: "Marvelous."

Gamadge turned his head. A youngish woman had come out on *her* balcony, and was also leaning on the rail. She smiled at him. She had a goodnatured, plain face with prominent features, prominent gray eyes, and brown hair fashionably done up in rolls and curls. She wore navy-blue slacks, blue-and-red sandals, a white silk shirt, and large gold earrings. On her muscular forearms were many bangles.

Gamadge said: "Please excuse my costume."

"I don't think we ought to bother about conventional clothes in these days," said the stranger.

"Still, I'm rather reactionary about going around in braces and no collar."

"Don't mind me. I think it's marvelous."

"What is?" smiled Gamadge.

"Men being here." The stranger gave a high, metallic laugh. "My name's Pender, Irene Pender."

"Mine's Gamadge, Henry Gamadge."

"The joke is that I thought there wouldn't be a soul at the Inn this time except Miss Crabbe and me. And this morning in come four men!"

"And a lady came."

"Well, anyway, she doesn't play golf. Perhaps she doesn't even play bridge!"

"I wouldn't count on that if I were you. So many do play bridge."

"Especially these oldfashioned women. But I don't believe women like Mrs. Maxwell play anything. They just get their man, and then they don't do a thing for the rest of their lives, but sit around and hang on to him."

"Very selfish."

"Anyway, the rest of you haven't any wives."

"So far as you know."

"I mean not here."

"Why do you come to such a quiet spot, if I may ask, Miss Pender?"

"Well, I'm from Uhiuh; but I have relatives in Springfield, and when it gets too dull at home I come East. But Springfield was terrible, and I got one of my silly old nervous breakdowns. So I ran over to the Crab Apple. I've come before when I had a breakdown. The Crab Apple always cures me. Don't you think golf is a cure all, Mr. Gamadge?"

"As long as one can lift a club."

"I can do that, still; I used to be local champion at home. But it's not such fun playing alone," said Miss Pender wistfully, "and now even Miss Crabbe can't play much, she's so busy in the Inn. Gin rummy in the evenings! It's as bad as home. Miss

Crabbe doesn't introduce guests, she says they ought to have their privacy; but at home it was all right for the local woman champion to challenge men to play golf."

"Of course. You must play a man's game."

"I did once. And I won the State tournament at bridge, once," said Miss Pender with pathetic eagerness.

"I don't know why anybody with your resources should have nervous breakdowns."

"It's dreadful at home since the war. Nothing but men going away, and I crash when I do war-work."

"If you don't like a job," said Gamadge, "it takes a lot of doggedness not to crash."

"It's all right for the *younger* girls. They travel, believe me!"

"You're wasting yourself. Why don't you cut loose and come to New York? You'd find plenty to do there."

"But I crash."

"You won't crash in New York. You won't knit or make bandages, you'll entertain at one of the clubs or canteens; and if you have a little extra money to spend on extra stuff for the boys to eat and drink you'll be the most popular woman in the town."

"I don't know a soul in New York."

Gamadge scribbled an address. "Here you are. They've just been starting a new group, and they've been calling my wife up to come and help, and pay for extra milk."

"Milk?"

"The warriors call for milk."

Miss Pender took the paper. "It's awfully nice of you—"

"Don't mew yourself up when you get there. Go to a big place where something's going on all the time. You must meet my friend Schenck. He's here with me. He has a bachelor apartment in New York, all full of gadgets."

This was going a little fast even for Miss Pender, but she kept up: "I'd certainly like to try New York."

"How about a little get-together this afternoon? Schenck and Boucher are asleep now, they're tired; but they'll wake up in time for tea and bridge. Would Miss Crabbe let us have it upstairs?"

"I should say so! I have a sitting-room. Marvelous."

"We'll ask Miss Crabbe to cut in. Only don't mention us to the Maxwells."

"Oh—do you know them?"

"Slightly."

"I don't. And I certainly don't want *her* at bridge!"

"Then if you should meet them at lunch, don't mention us. We'll surprise them at dinnertime."

"I'll tell Miss Crabbe you introduced yourself to me," said Miss Pender, looking arch. "*You* don't seem to worry much about your privacy!"

"No, I hate it."

They were still laughing over this subtle witticism when the houseman knocked at Gamadge's door. There was a telephone call. Gamadge excused himself to the now radiant Miss Pender, and went down to the booth. He came back, had his shower, and ate his lunch. After lunch he relaxed for an hour, and then tapped at Schenck's door.

There was a conference of an hour in Boucher's room; and when the three presented themselves at Miss Pender's sitting-room door she could not know that Boucher was not usually so silent, Schenck not always taut as a bow-string and talkative as a gramophone. As a rule they all played well: Boucher adored bridge, Schenck had an awful precision at the game and a deadly accuracy, Miss Pender certainly had not won a State tournament by inattention to the rules; but on this occasion form collapsed and crumbled. The players' states of mind were too much for it.

Boucher, always grave and exquisitely polite, more than once said 'arts when he meant the other red suit that stared him in the face. Gamadge played in a dream. Schenck and

Miss Pender, partners for the afternoon and kindred souls from the moment they met, leaned across the table to converse endlessly, their cards against their chests. Miss Pender forgot her cigarettes and let them roll from the ash tray to the rug, to her neighbors' knees; she dropped cards upon the floor, she sipped and spilled water. She and Schenck arranged their next meeting—to take place at his apartment in New York—from its date to its last detail of drink and food. They were entranced by each other's bounce and vivacity.

Miss Crabbe came in with the tea; was prevailed upon to play Gamadge's hand, and did so competently. She seemed pleased with the party; and if she thought the three men an ill-assorted trio she did not show that she thought so. She looked benevolently upon Schenck and Miss Pender, and at Boucher with interest.

At last she said that she ought to be going down to see what was going on in the kitchen.

"Miss Crabbe," said Gamadge, "I have a bottle of pretty fair whiskey with me. Could you be prevailed upon to join us in a highball?"

Miss Crabbe required no urging, and rang for ice. Gamadge mixed drinks, distributed them, and waited until they had been absorbed and might be supposed to have taken effect; then he ventured on:

"Miss Crabbe, I have a confession to make, an apology to tender, and a favor to ask."

Miss Crabbe put down her cigarette. "I knew it!"

"That we were not a week-end golfing party?"

Boucher said gently: "Madame would know it at a glance."

"I liked every one of you," said Miss Crabbe.

"Let me introduce us properly," said Gamadge. "Mr. Boucher is a distinguished ex-inspector of the Sûreté Générale of Paris."

"I knew he was somebody!"

"Mr. Schenck is an agent of the Federal Bureau of Investigation."

Miss Pender sank back in her chair, looked fondly at Schenck, and murmured: "Marvelous."

"You're not after spies, are you?" inquired Miss Crabbe calmly. "We have none here, not even in the kitchen."

"We are not after spies. I am Henry Gamadge, a nobody; or let me offer myself modestly as the conscientious citizen."

Miss Crabbe sat up suddenly. "But why on earth—don't say it's the Maxwells!"

"I told you I didn't like her," said Miss Pender.

"The horrid truth is," continued Gamadge, "that the lady is not Mrs. Maxwell."

Miss Crabbe rose slowly to her feet: "I can deal with that!"

"You can't deal with it, Miss Crabbe; we're here to deal with Mr. and Mrs. Maxwell."

"They'll leave tonight!"

"They'll leave, I promise you."

Miss Crabbe slowly resumed her seat. "Don't tell me," she said, fixing Gamadge through her spectacles, "that you three men came up here to arrest these people just because they aren't married to each other. It's more serious."

"It's serious."

"Are the police coming to the Inn?"

"That's what Schenck and Boucher and I want to avoid; it's shocking that the Inn should be involved at all. I don't think it need be; it was only a point of meeting and departure for this lady and gentleman, and they won't have been here a day. What I should like to propose is this: you and Miss Pender have your dinner upstairs, and keep the servants out of the dining-room. When the Maxwells have gone down to dinner, have their bags packed and brought out to the side porch, and leave the rest to us."

Miss Crabbe said dryly: "That's easy."

"The Crab Apple won't get any more publicity than we can help; it's just your tough luck that Mr. Maxwell ever heard of it. Did he ever say how he did come to hear of it?"

"Through friends. He and Mr. Crenshaw came on the first, and they had the suite the Maxwells have now. I liked Mr. Crenshaw much the better of the two."

Irene Pender giggled. "You liked Mr. Maxwell well enough! You said he was interesting."

"I said he was interesting," snapped Miss Crabbe. "I didn't say I liked him. Dr. Samuel Johnson was interesting, but I shouldn't have liked him at all. He wouldn't have given me any reason to."

Gamadge, after struggling for a moment with the idea of Miss Crabbe and Dr. Johnson in social juxtaposition, gave it up and went on:

"They were here from June first to June fifteenth, you said."

"And then they were going up to Vermont. Mr. Crenshaw sat out on their porch—that suite has a porch—most of the time, and read. Mr. Maxwell played a little golf with the caddies; some of our caddies are as good as a pro."

"No doubt. Mr. Crenshaw didn't strike you as a very sick man?"

"Just rather languid."

"Melancholy?"

"I never saw a man yet who could be cheerful when he wasn't well. Then Mr. Crenshaw felt better, and they left for Vermont."

"You're sure they left for that reason? No other people coming to the Inn at that time?"

"Some people *were* coming."

"I suggest this because Mr. Crenshaw wasn't likely to be feeling better. And Mr. Maxwell told you before he left that he would be coming back?"

"With his wife," said Miss Crabbe indignantly. "He didn't

know when they might be coming. Yesterday he telephoned me from the Long Valley Inn at Unionboro, and said Mrs. Maxwell would be up that evening, and he'd join her today, and he hoped they could have the same suite."

"Asked first if there were other people here?"

"Yes; I thought he was asking because he wanted the suite, you know. I told him we only had one guest—Irene Pender. Mrs. Maxwell arrived, all excited to be seeing her husband again. She told me she'd come all the way from Texas, and that Mr. Maxwell had been with a sick friend, helping him settle an estate. I can't get over it. You'd have thought they'd been married a long time, by the way she talked—I was completely taken in! Such a quiet, dignified—"

"Just one of those dear sweet oldfashioned things," observed Miss Pender. "You ought to have seen her slide past me on the stairs—oh, so exclusive!"

"But she didn't seem nervous," said Miss Crabbe. "Neither of them seemed nervous."

"They're not nervous. Mr. Maxwell," said Gamadge, smiling, "is never nervous."

"Well, I'm thankful I never have to see them again. Or will I?" She frowned at Gamadge.

"You may. I hope not."

"So do I. Irene, we'll have dinner here. And those bags will be packed and taken down and out, Mr. Gamadge; you can count on me!"

"What a sport you are."

Schenck had been conducting a low-voiced conversation with Irene Pender. He lingered to finish it when Gamadge and Boucher followed Miss Crabbe into the hall.

"Nerves of steel, has that one," murmured Boucher, glancing back. "No imagination. He has all the luck."

"You have the imagination, Boucher. And I have nerves, all right; but not of steel."

"Twice I declared 'arts when it was diamonds."

"You leave the hearts to them. I have a feeling that my wife is going to have her circle of acquaintance widened. She's made some unlikely friends since she married me."

"If I may judge by my own experience, she will make the best of Miss Pender."

CHAPTER EIGHTEEN

Reunion

AT HALF PAST SEVEN a striking couple entered the dining-room of the Crab Apple Inn, and found that they had the place to themselves. Candles were lighted on their corner table, but no servant was to be seen. The slim, blond man walked with his dark companion across the room, and he held her chair for her. He was well dressed in tweeds, but she wore a plain, expensive evening costume with a smart jacket. Her hair was piled high. Ear rings gleamed in her small ears, and there was a big diamond pin on the lapel of the silk coat.

"I hope," he said, "that Miss Crabbe hasn't lost her only waitress."

"Oh, no; they're just late as usual."

He took his seat opposite her, with his back to the room. "Well, at least we can't complain of the crowd! But in a day or so we'll be in a livelier place."

"I snubbed that tiresome girl this morning; that Pender girl."

"Ghastly type. Well, the Crab Apple is all my friend on the Sandsea golf course said it would be; but I shan't be playing golf!" He added: "Not sorry for a good long rest."

She smiled at him. "You've been wonderful."

"So have you. The thing is that it's all over. Isn't it fun to think that not one living soul knows where we are? We're alone on earth together! At last. No more worry."

"I couldn't stand any more of it. Darling…"

"Yes?"

"I can't help thinking about that Fisher girl."

He sat back. "Now don't begin it all over again!"

"But *could* that Billig—"

"It was a hold-up, it must have been a hold-up. Billig wouldn't lose his head like that; and for nothing! She knew nothing; she told that fellow Gamadge nothing."

"Billig may have thought—"

"Even if he did, what had he to get into such a stew about?"

"You said you thought he might take drugs."

"Because he needed the two thousand, and lived in such a hole. That's why I thought so. I don't know so."

"But if he takes drugs he *may* lose his head. He may have lost it and killed that girl. It's such a coincidence. I nearly died when I heard it like that—no preparation."

"I bet you didn't give a thing away."

"Gamadge was there; it was frightful."

"The Fisher girl consulted him about some book or autograph; just as he said. It's his business."

"You don't think anything's queer; you never do."

"Yes, I do. I think it was queer that he went to the apartment house on Thursday afternoon and inquired about the flat."

"There's nothing funny about it if you're right, and Idelia Fisher consulted him professionally. Of course they talked about the whole case—"

"I like your *calling* it a case!"

"When they went up to the hospital together they talked about that poor Mr. Crenshaw; and Gamadge may really have wanted a flat for the summer."

"Yes, but how did *she* know about the apartment?"

"Asked at the post-office in Stonehill. There was no secret about it, you say. You think I'm nervous! You're imagining all kinds of things."

"I wasn't the one who imagined that Idelia Fisher consulted Gamadge about the Shakespeare."

"I still think she did."

"Why did she?"

"If I knew I shouldn't be wondering about it."

Their voices had taken on an edge. After a short silence he said: "Lucky I brought that bottle of gin along. I don't know where we should be if we hadn't had a cocktail." He smiled. "We ought to have had several more. Can't we forget all this? We have pretty good proof that there's nothing in it; if there had been, don't you think we'd have known it before now?"

There was another pause. Then she said in a dry voice: "I wonder if we're going to do this all our lives.'

"Do what?"

"Go over it and over it."

"No; because we'll be far away. Billig won't tell; not he! I know that type. I saw twenty apartments before I chose that one, with no doctor in it, and the nearest doctor a broken-down M.D. around the corner. I worked it all out like a problem in chess. I watched Billig, and I saw the kind of patients he had. I don't know why he's on his beam-ends, but it's something serious. Blackmail? Or perhaps he *is* mixed up in the drug traffic and taking a drug himself. That runs to money."

"But if he takes drugs—he may have—he may collapse any time, and tell."

He smiled. "Are we back there again?"

"I wish I'd asked that Humbert exactly what Gamadge said when he first came to the apartment."

"Instead of which you let it go."

"I was afraid Humbert would think I worried about it."

"You're worrying, all right. Shall we make a vow not to say another thing about it? Stop spoiling the fun?"

"Yes."

"Good. That's settled. We pulled the thing off, I don't think any job was ever pulled off so neatly as this job was. It's no fault of ours if our late friend stumbled across the Fisher girl at Stonehill. I'd pay money to know how he did stumble across her. It must have been those times while I was down in the village. Sly of him, very sly, to keep it to himself."

She said rather viciously: "You said you understood him."

There was something vicious in his face, too, when he replied: "Knew better than to run any risks with me, anyway. But there's an element—the X in any human chemical combination. You can't depend on it. Variable. Well, he's made a lot of trouble and cost this Fisher girl—" He stopped, and looked at her guiltily.

"You do think Dr. Billig killed her! You do!"

They stared at each other. Then he said gently: "How about that vow we made? And where—" his tone changed, he lifted a fork and struck a bell-note on his tumbler—"where the devil is the waitress?"

The clear sound of silver on glass might have been a knell to raise a spirit, by the look on her face as she gazed beyond him at the doorway; he turned his head, and he too was frozen and rigid; a man of stone.

Schenck, Gamadge and Boucher came directly up to the table; Schenck went around the woman to sit between her and her companion; Boucher sat down in the chair opposite; Gamadge remained standing; he looked down at the man known as Maxwell with a smile.

"Good evening," he said. "May we join you?"

Maxwell seemed to be endowed with immense self confidence; it did not quite desert him even now. He replied, after moistening his lips: "I don't know you. What is all this?"

"But Miss Daker knows me. Perhaps she'll introduce me?"

Lucette Daker, in her new coiffure and long skirt, her earrings and her brilliant make-up, seemed much older than she had looked in New York; but her expression, furious and terrified, was what altered her most. She glared speechless at Gamadge, and then turned the same basilisk eye on the man opposite her.

"Since she doesn't care to introduce me," said Gamadge, "let me introduce myself—though it isn't really necessary. My name is Gamadge, and these are my friends Schenck and Boucher. You and Miss Daker may have seen Schenck at Stonehill, and you probably noticed Boucher, Mr. Maxwell, on the bus. Not yesterday's bus, you know; not the bus Miss Daker came down from Unionboro on."

Maxwell tapped his fingers gently on the table-cloth. Then he said: "You'd better go upstairs, Lucette; I'll settle this. It's an outrage, but I suppose even a gang of private detectives can be made to understand that it won't be worth their while to press a morals charge; and that's the only charge they could possibly hold us on."

Gamadge said: "I really wouldn't go, Miss Daker. You have rights, even if you did treat poor Mr. Judd Binney in a most shocking way. He was your alibi, I see that—and Mr. Maxwell's. We weren't to look beyond Mr. Binney when you faded from the scene."

She had risen, and now screamed at him: "We quarrelled yesterday. We quarrelled!"

"Nonsense; he has gone off on his ship thinking that if he comes back you'll marry him. He was to find a letter saying you'd changed your mind, and asking him to forget you. You were going to write to your aunt, though, as you told me, and say you'd married him. But I wasn't convinced by poor Binney, you know; people like you are not likely to throw themselves away on Binneys; they hunt bigger game."

Maxwell said: "Lucette, you don't have to listen—" but she shrieked at him: "You said I'd be safe! You said you'd take care of me!"

He looked at her silently; the basilisk had turned his pale, stricken face to a death-mask.

Gamadge shook his head at her: "You mustn't put too much faith in human promises, Miss Daker. And you've been awfully bad for him, you know; you turned him into a murderer. He killed Idelia Fisher, and if he'd had a chance he would have killed me afterwards. Didn't you know?"

The man came to life at that. He interrupted harshly: "What do you mean? I was at Stonehill."

"Not that night. They didn't know at Stonehill that you were ever away between the twenty-second and yesterday afternoon, but it was the simplest thing in the world for you to drive down by devious routes, park your car somewhere in Unionboro, and take the express to New York. You saw Billig a few minutes before I did on Wednesday night; you heard that Idelia and I had been at the hospital, and were perhaps even than at Buckley's; you went after us both within the next hour. You missed me, and you couldn't try again; you had to catch the 12:01 to Unionboro. My friends here saw you while you were on your way home to the Crenshaw house—they got to Stonehill a few minutes after you did. I couldn't go up, you know; you saw me with Idelia on Wednesday night after we left Buckley's; if you'd caught a glimpse of me at Stonehill you'd have been scared off, and we might have lost you. Or would you have shot me on sight?"

Maxwell pulled himself together; he raised his eyes to the girl who was staring at him. "This is what they call shock tactics, Lucette; we mustn't let them stampede us. There's absolutely no evidence that I was ever in New York after the twenty-second. There's no evidence at all."

Gamadge said: "Billig—"

"Billig!" Maxwell laughed.

"Billig states that you called on him last Wednesday night, paid him one thousand dollars (the remaining half of his fee), and heard of Idelia Fisher for the first time. Not knowing what you were capable of, or that you had reason to commit murder, he gave you her address, and the information—just received over the telephone from Mr. Thompson of St. Damian's—that she and I were on our way to Buckley's. I may add that Dr. Billig himself is not involved in the murder. He has an effective alibi for the murder; his time is fully accounted for. Idelia was killed within half an hour of the time I found her body, and during that half hour Billig was on his way to the Jeremiah H. Wood Home, in the East Fifties. They know when he got there."

Maxwell said loudly: "Inference." His light eyes, just showing beneath pale lashes, were fixed on Gamadge's with cold intensity.

"Inference," agreed Gamadge. "I am fully aware of the fact that you may never be tried for that murder at all. But as you know very well, you can be tried for a felony—since we've caught you, and if we can hang on to you until Mrs. Crenshaw gets here from New York."

The light eyes blinked and shifted. Lucette Daker got up and stood clinging to the edge of the table. Her lips formed the words: "New York?"

"I called her up yesterday afternoon and asked her to stay on," said Gamadge. "Called her up from the Grand Central, you know."

She gazed at him. "That time you—that time—"

"I'm afraid so."

"Even *then* you—" she had found her voice, and it expressed something like horror.

"I'm afraid so, Miss Daker. I was trying to find out who had killed my client. Well, as I said, your friend may never stand trial for that murder; but he'll stand trial for the felony, and we'll hold him now on a Federal charge. Mr. Schenck is an agent of the F.B.I., and can make the arrest."

Maxwell asked roughly: "What Federal charge? What are you talking about? There can't be one."

"There is one, and in less shocking circumstances the fact would be laughable. Your grave error. In the course of building up a fraud you falsified or conspired to falsify documents; that's the felony. And for that purpose you used the United States mails; don't you remember your letter to Mr. Humbert, Mr. Maxwell? That's the Federal offense. The letter was mailed in Stonehill on the third of July."

Maxwell's thin lips moved. "Frame-up."

"But who would frame you, Mr. Maxwell?"

Maxwell seemed to huddle down into his chair; but that effect was caused only by a narrowing of the shoulders, a drawing in of the legs and feet. Otherwise he did not move.

"Such a beautiful, such a perfect plan," said Gamadge. "Why did you ruin it by lending the dying man your volume of Shakespeare, Crenshaw? He was your cousin, wasn't he? I thought there must have been a family likeness; it would have looked suspicious to cremate him, and somebody might have described the body to your wife."

Lucette Daker gasped: "That girl—I knew she brought you that book for some reason!"

"Don't waste resentment on her," said Gamadge. "If I had had no more information than what she could give me I shouldn't be here now. It was the book itself that told me the story. The dead man wasn't the owner—couldn't be the owner; he was a reader of Shakespeare; he wouldn't have brought that

Shakespeare with him on his long journey—a bound, battered, closely printed volume out of a family set.

"But if he had? If I was wrong? No: I wasn't wrong about the ownership of that Shakespeare. If it was his only Shakespeare, why was it as fresh between its disintegrating covers as when it had first come from the printers, one hundred and four years ago?

"The man posing as Howard Crenshaw wasn't Howard Crenshaw; he was somebody—one of those cousins from Omaha?—who had borrowed a volume of Shakespeare from the Crenshaw library; a volume stamped with a Crenshaw name. But Howard Crenshaw must have been close at hand; to sign papers in New York and Stonehill, to sign checks, to write home. Was Pike Howard Crenshaw? I thought so."

Crenshaw said: "There's no motive."

"No financial motive, none. But there are others even more powerful. How does one get rid of a blameless wife who won't divorce? Only by death; so when your cousin came to you, and asked your help, and told you that he was dying of leukemia, you decided to be the one to die. You shouldn't have trusted him not to talk to strangers, Crenshaw; you shouldn't have lent him that book out of your library at Sundown. You should have drowned it first, *deeper than did ever plummet sound*."

Crenshaw brought up his right knee; the table, with all its glass and silverware crashed against Schenck, but it was not Schenck, after all, who had the gun. Boucher had it, and he shot Crenshaw's pistol out of his hand.

CHAPTER NINETEEN

Off the Record

D R. FLORIAN BILLIG was profoundly sunk in Gamadge's deepest and widest chair, with a frosted tumbler on the table beside him and a cigar in his thick fingers; but he looked very much cast down. So did Gamadge, who sat on the chesterfield facing him.

"It was abominable, Doctor," he said. "I hated doing it. But if I hadn't, you never would have screwed yourself up to telling me, and we had to have your evidence."

"I tried to tell you often enough."

"Don't worry about Geegan and his operatives, by the way; they fully understand that it was all an unfortunate mistake."

Billig said: "Geegan and his operatives will know all about me soon enough." He sighed, rolled sideways, and extracted a letter from his pocket. He opened it, and after a glance at Gamadge through the upper half of his bifocals, read it aloud in a booming voice:

My dear Dr. Billig,

I am in possession of Charge Coin Number 152593, property of the lady now going under the name of Dodson. Stengel's department store will have her real name and her former address. Stengel's will not give it to me, but they will if required to do so give it to the police.

I have no wish to apply to the police. I do not believe that your part in the Pike-Crenshaw affair was criminal, and I should like if possible to keep you out of the case. I cannot even attempt to do so unless I know your motives and have your story.

Please take a night to think it over. Tomorrow at noon I shall telegraph you where to reach me by telephone, and I shall hope to hear from you soon afterwards.

I must advise you that I have operatives working on the matter, and that you will not be able to remove yourself—or anyone else—from the city without my knowledge.

> *Very truly yours,*
> *HENRY GAMADGE.*

Billig folded the letter, leaned forward, handed it to Gamadge, and sank back in his chair.

"Blackmail," he said, "is a serious crime. You had better burn that communication, Mr. Gamadge."

"Thanks. I will." Gamadge snapped on his lighter, and watched the typed sheet curl to ashes.

"Of course I had no choice," said Billig. "I had been expecting something of the sort ever since Mrs. Lubic informed me of your visit to the Wood Home. Was the—er—incident of the handbag that same afternoon part of your campaign?"

"I'm afraid so."

"That poor girl—my wife; I always think of her as my wife, I always shall; and to this day, Gamadge, whether you can believe it or whether you can't, I'd rather be in the same room with her than with any other living creature—there's still a charge out against her for shoplifting. She's dying. Her brain's going, but it's not too far gone to register what an arrest is. I want her to go out in peace, and I don't want a scandal. She comes from—comes from a very good family."

"Anybody can see that."

"But you should have seen her when she was young. You should—" he looked up at Gamadge from under heavy brows— "you should have seen me. No beauty, you know, and what a background. Memory shies from it. A brilliant young fellow, though, well thought of in his profession. Her people would never have allowed her to marry me, naturally; and she had no money of her own. She had the spirit and the heart to run away with me.

"Of course it didn't last—for her. It was hard going, and I wasn't her sort; and when the novelty wore off she swung back to what she had been brought up to.

"I gave her a divorce, naturally, but the fellow was no good. They weren't together long. She'd gone down a little by that time, and soon she was in bad trouble. I was able to get her out of it, but I'm still paying that bill and there were others. I never could seem to get ahead.

"This shoplifting—I was at my wits' end. I had to hide her. The Wood Home—even the little place in Queens—were more than I could afford, and when Pike came along on the afternoon of the sixth of July I was wondering what to do.

"I knew there was something wrong, of course; a man in Crenshaw's circumstances wouldn't have sent out and got *me* if there hadn't been something wrong; and when I told him what was the matter with him I knew he'd been diagnosed before, and that the incurable nature of the disease was no news to him.

You can't fool a man who's been in practice as long as I have, and doomed as many people. When he pretended that my news was news, I asked myself what I was being hired to do."

"Barton Crenshaw," said Gamadge, "had been diagnosed in May—immediately before he went to San Francisco from Omaha and appealed to his rich cousin Howard—whom he had never liked, and whom he hadn't seen for at least twenty-five years. We have details from Lucette Daker."

"Barton Crenshaw," said Billig, "couldn't face a charity ward in a hospital and a pauper's grave. I don't much blame him."

"I'm not inclined to be too hard on his memory myself. He was the last of his branch of the family, a fastidious, easy-living man who'd earned a good income by research, but who hadn't saved a penny. When that ghastly illness developed, Howard Crenshaw was his last resort. Howard offered him all the luxuries; but when they were offered as the price of compounding a fraud, Barton wasn't as grateful as he would otherwise have been. He succumbed to the temptation, but he didn't live up to the bargain as Howard did. He cheated; and he blamed himself for cheating."

"I can see why he succumbed to the temptation," said Billig. "He foresaw—what? An indefinite sojourn in some hospital; no luxuries and precious few comforts; there's a shortage of nurses now. Sick, alone, and poor—I can see the temptation to escape that."

"And I can see why he broke his promise and made a friend. In Idelia Fisher he found his last chance to be admired; the last build-up for his self-esteem. He could tell himself, poor devil, that if Idelia admired him there must be something in him after all. There was, of course: literary taste," said Gamadge, smiling.

"The fraud," said Billig, "wasn't financial. Mrs. Howard Crenshaw lost no money by it; or none that she could possibly have expected to get."

"And Howard told the sick man that he was merely escaping from life with a mean and selfish woman—an intolerable life. Of course he *had* asked for a divorce—many times. Mrs. Crenshaw didn't permit that humiliating fact to be known in Sundown, California!"

"They value their position in the community," said Billig, rotating his thumbs while he pondered the Mrs. Crenshaws. "They don't like the status of divorced wife."

"And if Crenshaw had simply left her she wouldn't have given him a moment's peace; she would have had him hounded to the ends of the earth—which are not as far away now as they would be if there were no war. Howard Crenshaw couldn't have set up with Lucette Daker as Mr. Maxwell, or rather as Mr. Strong. He had more money, of course, than his wife imagined—ten times more. He'd sold the business more profitably than she knew, he'd saved and speculated. His separate account is in Georgia, under the name of Strong. Quite a catch, was Mr. Crenshaw; but he wasn't getting younger, and Lucette Daker wasn't the kind to wait for him or any man, and she would only live with him if she could be accepted as his wife."

"He had been in love with her from the time she came into the house?"

"There are ways of being in love. You haven't seen her, Doctor; it's a type that can do fearful damage to a man unless he's allergic to it."

"I gather that you are allergic to it?"

"Yes. I don't like them *quite* so oldfashioned, you know; I like them not quite so primitive. It's the oldest fashion in the world, Lucette Daker's."

"We are cynical?"

"You should have seen her turn on him the moment the plot went wrong; it wasn't human. I'll never forget it; never forget his face. He thought she loved him. He had had illusions about her, and yet—how keenly he had judged his wife! He knew perfectly what her reaction would be to the news of his illness and death. They were normal; she was aware, if we were not, that her husband had had no reason to consider her feelings; she thought he'd been spiting her. She was angry when I saw her, but she didn't show great surprise. And he knew she wouldn't waste time on anything but the money end of it—he knew very well that she wouldn't ask to see his body, or even go to the funeral."

"Why did he leave her so much in his will?"

"It was an old will, made when they were first married; he really had nobody else to leave money to, until Lucette Daker came; and by that time he had plenty more. The unchanged will would allay suspicion; Mrs. Crenshaw wouldn't inquire beyond it."

"I suppose Barton Crenshaw presented himself at the bank here, but Howard was on hand to sign checks."

"And documents. No checks were signed at the bank, and when Ferris came up on the afternoon of the twenty-first with the cash balance, Barton had a check for the exact amount— made out and signed by Howard—in his writing pad. He wrote a check himself, and switched them. That cash balance satisfied everybody here; no questions asked."

Billig glanced at him. Then he said: "Miss Daker has done a lot of talking."

"She'll say anything to get out of standing trial as an accomplice to the fraud. Mrs. Crenshaw would probably have her boiled in oil if she could, but she won't be; she'll be State's witness."

"Barton Crenshaw didn't know of her existence?"

"He only suspected it later, when he had time to study his cousin Howard and his motives. *Cherchez la femme.* Lucette Daker must have come into the conversation—how could a man obsessed as Crenshaw was keep her entirely out of it?"

"It's odd that a woman of Mrs. Crenshaw's type didn't suspect."

"Lucette Daker had many admirers, and you ought to have heard her talk about her poor dear Uncle Howard! But he wasn't even a step-uncle, and I was looking for the woman, and she seemed to be cutting herself off rather suddenly and at a crucial moment from her past. Nor did she behave as though her happiness depended on poor Binney. The enthusiasm was all on his side, I do assure you."

Billig said: "Your powers of observation are greater than mine. I thought that Pike and Crenshaw were hiding from the law, of course; embezzlement, some form of thievery or fraud, I didn't know. The sick man didn't look like a swindler, but then I didn't think I was a swindler until I took the two thousand dollars for helping them keep out of contact with the world—and asking no questions. When Pike came to me on the evening of the twenty-eighth—with the rest of my pay, you know—I felt in duty bound to tell him that inquiries were being made; I gave him Idelia Fisher's name, and your name, and her address, and the information that you were going to Buckley's. I had been called up by the hospital. Mr. Thompson, the night supervisor, was interested. I should have seen that the man I knew as Pike was staggered by my news; it was the first he'd heard of Idelia Fisher; he must have been thunderstruck. But he seemed no more than mildly interested. The truth is that the thought of my own venality—and the thought that this man knew it—was so hideous to me that I wasn't paying much attention to him. I sent him directly to her; I condemned her to death. And I kept silence afterwards. I spent many unprofitable hours, I assure you, telling myself that the papers were right—that it was a hold-up."

"You could only guess that it wasn't. As a matter of fact he had plenty of time to catch us when we left Buckley's, identify us to his own satisfaction—he had seen Idelia at Stonehill—and follow us to the drugstore. He saw me head uptown, but of course stuck to her; what mightn't Barton Crenshaw have told her, what mightn't she have told me? They must have travelled across town on the same bus; it didn't matter if she saw him—she would have been very glad of a message from Howard Crenshaw! But I don't think she ever did see him. She was unlocking the door, and she was struck down from behind.

"As for me—he had to make the attempt on me, but he didn't really worry about me much. He didn't really worry much about her; but he killed her. That's the ugly thing about him—he'd kill rather than run the faintest risk."

After a silence Billig said: "The ugly thing about me is that I wanted that poor soul at the Wood Home to have two thousand dollars more than I wanted the truth about the Fisher girl's death. I drove straight down after you left me and put it in her handbag. You know why she hung on to it like that? Because that was where she used to put the stuff she lifted from the shops. She had nothing to hide any more, but sometimes she thought she had. They're very decent down there; I've known Mrs. Lubic a long time. She'd have spent the two thousand on her if anything happened to me.

"Well." Billig heaved himself out of his chair. "I always knew no good would come of the Pike-Crenshaw business. When you walked in on me that night I knew it was all up with me—don't ask me why. Guilty conscience? I simply felt it in my bones. I'm a doctor, and I diagnosed Barton Crenshaw correctly and treated him properly, and it wasn't my business to inquire into his private life; but I took twenty times my reasonable fee for keeping my mouth shut and protecting him from questions and outside contacts; and I didn't go to the police after the Fisher girl was killed. When they get me into court I won't get the benefit of any doubt on the witness stand; Crenshaw's counsel will say I was in on the racket, and why shouldn't he think so? I'm done for, and I deserve to be."

Gamadge had not risen. He said, looking up at the other earnestly: "Don't give up yet, Doctor."

"No? You won't save me," said Billig, smiling down at him,

"and you won't send Howard Crenshaw to the electric chair. But perhaps you'll be satisfied with the penitentiary for him? Perhaps Idelia Fisher would be?"

"If Idelia was vindictive," said Gamadge, "she would have been satisfied when she saw the look on Crenshaw's face when that furious little creature leaned across the table at the Crab Apple Inn and screamed at him. And he'd committed murder for her. She was shocked silly, of course; I meant her to be. That's why I let them come down to dinner so complacently— to shock her afterwards into turning against him. But his shock went deeper. He would have shot her first, and then himself; when that didn't come off he was like a dead man. Went off with us without another word, and never looked at her again."

Billig said, turning away: "Well, I'll be on hand when you want me."

Gamadge rose. "Don't go yet, Doctor. There's the door bell; a man on business, but he won't stay long. I want to talk something over with you. Look here: I apologize in advance for suggesting such a thing to a man of your qualities, but if the worst should come to the worst, I need a laboratory man badly. Mine's at the wars, and when he comes back he's going to marry and set up for himself. I feel like a fool to offer you such a job, but temporarily—and the lab's quite a nice little hole. You might care to go down now and look at it? Toy with the microspectrograph?"

Billig stood for a few moments looking at nothing. Then he said: "I should like very much to see your laboratory, Mr. Gamadge."

They went down in the elevator. Gamadge took the doctor into the laboratory by the back way, switched on lights, and pulled covers from groups of apparatus. He said: "Just make yourself at home, Doctor."

"I am at home."

CHAPTER TWENTY

Gamadge Is Not Bored

WHEN GAMADGE CAME BACK upstairs to the library he found Detective-Lieutenant Durfee there, making himself comfortable. His feet were up on the chesterfield, and he had poured himself a drink. He said: "Excuse my not rising."

Gamadge sat down in the chair his other guest had occupied, and lighted a cigarette. "Durfee," he said, "what can we do for poor old Billig?"

"Did you offer him the job?"

"He's down there now. It's a frightful shame. He wouldn't have touched the two thousand for himself, there's some indigent sick relative."

"He was a diagnostician. These specialists charge horrible fees—couldn't he make out that two thousand was usual?"

"Two thousand dollars for an analysis any hospital pathologist will do for five dollars?"

Durfee settled his shoulders into the cushions of the chesterfield. He said: "We know all about Mrs. Dodson and the

Jeremiah Wood Home, you know. We know when he put her there."

Gamadge looked blank.

"That shoplifting charge was dropped long ago," continued Durfee. "Nobody's going to bother Mrs. Dodson; she was as mad as a hatter when she committed the last theft—costume jewelry to the amount of one dollar and seventy-seven cents. Of course she was a repeater; but we won't bother her now. Where's 'home'?"

"'Home'?" Gamadge was staring.

"Where she wants to go."

"Billig says it was a brick house in the East Thirties, torn down the year after the Hotel Windsor fire. She ran away from it to marry the promising young Dr. Billig, but I think she must have been happy there once."

"You can tell him not to worry about *her*, anyway."

"I shall." Gamadge, still slightly agape, made himself a highball.

"As I make it out," Durfee went on, thoughtfully gazing at the polychromatic ceiling, "we wouldn't want Billig at all if we didn't need him to establish Pike's presence in New York on the night of July twenty-eighth. He didn't *know* the sick man was a criminal hiding from justice—he only thought so. And nobody thinks less of a doctor because he don't nose around trying to find out his patient's business."

"That's so."

"It was only a guess on Billig's part, wasn't it, that Crenshaw had been diagnosed before? Nothing to show for an earlier diagnosis?"

"No."

"Nothing unethical about letting the patient stay in the apartment until a week before his death? Nothing unethical in not giving him the treatments if he didn't want them?"

"Not a thing."

"We have the hospital doctors and nurses to swear it was

a natural death—from acute leukemia. They'll swear that nothing could have saved the patient. As for the Fisher girl's murder, we have no atom of proof that Billig ever connected it with Pike; and as for the evidence that he gave Pike the girl's address, that's corroborative; it isn't worth a nickel by itself. As for the two thousand dollars," finished Durfee, "a patient can take a fancy to a doctor and leave him a legacy; why not give it to him beforehand, in cash?"

"Why not?" repeated Gamadge.

"I'm just explaining that we don't think we'll call in Billig; and the other side certainly won't call him—he wouldn't do *them* any good!"

Gamadge's mouth fell open, but he said nothing.

"In the first place," Durfee went on, "we think we've got Pike placed in New York without the doctor's evidence."

"You have?"

"We found a little garage in Unionboro where he left his car early on the morning of July twenty-eight before he caught the day express down. We can't place him on it, he travelled by day coach; or that's what we think he did. But the conductor on the 12:01 that night positively identifies him."

"That's rather too good to be true."

"I don't know. He was disguised, but the man picked him out."

"I hope you can make it stick," said Gamadge. "Those identifications aren't much use in a murder case."

"Too bad you didn't get a look at him in the hallway downstairs on the famous night," said Durfee.

"I thought I'd better go on living."

"You had it settled in your mind that it was Pike, even then?"

"And that Pike was Howard Crenshaw."

"On account of that book. I always," said Durfee indulgently, his hands clasped behind his head and one knee over the other, "I always like your rigmaroles."

"Well, that's what you would have thought it was. I had no

case, I had no evidence but the Shakespeare that Crenshaw was Pike. There was nobody I knew of nearer than California who could say that the dead man wasn't Howard Crenshaw, and I didn't know who he was. I had to collect evidence, and I had to keep Howard Crenshaw from getting lost. He was disguised, and he had another personality waiting to be stepped into—I was certain he had. I couldn't risk losing a minute or giving him any thing to suspect."

"So you tied it in for Schenck."

"Schenck's satisfied. And little Boucher knew what I was up to the minute he heard the précis of the case."

"Then along came Mrs. Crenshaw."

"Who for all I knew was an accomplice in this peculiar game; but when I saw the niece, and heard about how the niece was going to take that night trip up to Vermont just to be at her uncle Howard's funeral, I thought perhaps I'd found the woman in the case.

"I let her go. Perhaps we could catch up with them some-where when they were feeling quite safe. I would present my case as complete, and perhaps she'd throw Crenshaw over to save her own skin. She didn't hesitate."

"So why are you looking so discouraged?"

Gamadge clashed ice in his tumbler. "Because we won't convict Crenshaw of killing my client. That's why."

"He was too smart for us." Durfee swung his foot, still eyeing the painted ceiling.

"We may prove he was in New York that night, and we may do it without Billig's evidence," continued Gamadge. "But we won't prove he committed the murder."

"You're right after him, aren't you?"

"Yes, I am. I never think of him except by his nickname."

"That's so, somebody did say Pike was a nickname."

"He was quite proud of it. He told Lucette Daker how he earned it when he and Barton and the gang were boys together in a little town near Omaha."

"Because when he hung on to something he wouldn't let go?"

"Deadly and remorseless, those fellows, aren't they, hanging on to the bait? When he and Barton came together in late May they decided that Barton should always call him Pike; in case he slipped up and called him by his right name, you know."

"Thought of everything, didn't he? Pretty smart guy, for an amateur."

"I wish you wouldn't keep on calling him smart," said Gamadge with some irritation.

"He was smart. He probably killed the girl with his own pistol—handy kind of blunt instrument to carry around in a pocket—and he must have got a lot of blood on it and on the glove he wore. No bloodstains, though. He must have taken the glove off and wrapped his hand in a handkerchief before he started to empty the handbag—had to empty it so we'd think it was a hold-up. He never left a fingerprint on or in the bag, and there isn't a spot of blood on that suit that was in the bag they packed up for you at the Crab Apple Inn."

"I know all that."

"You're not as much interested in these sordid details as we poor old pros are. We love them. He must have crammed all her stuff into his pocket—left-hand pocket, probably, to keep it separate from his own things—and when he got to a good place—up country somewhere?—he threw her things all away. All," said Durfee, slowly swinging his legs over the side of the chesterfield and sitting up, "but this."

He took a little wooden box out of his pocket, slid open the cover, and allowed Gamadge to look at a small white object that reposed within, under a protecting layer of glass.

Gamadge looked, and went on looking. The thing was rectangular, about an inch and a half wide by two inches long. It was slightly rolled at one end, and decorated with a large initial or a monogram.

"That stayed in his pocket," said Durfee. "He thought it was his paper of matches, and he often fingered it; but he never did take it out and open it and throw it away."

Gamadge said in a faint voice: "She showed it to me. It's her darning kit."

"She showed it to her landlady, too, and she showed it to the servant at the rooming house. Cute little thing. Nice glossy surface, it's got her fingerprints on it; and it's got his, too."

Gamadge shouted: "Durfee, you black-hearted something, why didn't you tell me at first?"

Durfee slid the wooden cover back, and replaced the box in his pocket. He said when he could speak: "I would have, but fingerprints bore you."

It was some time before Durfee, still choking and gasping, took himself off. Gamadge went down to the laboratory.

Dr. Billig turned from contemplation of photographic enlargements, very much as a weary old buffalo turns slowly to look at somebody who has come up to the bars of his pen.

"It's all right, Doctor."

"All right?"

"The police won't call you as a witness; they won't need you. The other side won't call you, for their own sake. With any luck, you're out of it. And there's no charge out against Mrs. Dodson."

Billig put a hand behind him and steadied himself. After a pause he said: "Mr. Gamadge."

"Doctor?"

"I should like to act henceforth as your consultant; if—if— it can be arranged on a friendly basis, no fees."

"No fees." Gamadge laughed.

"If I may have the freedom of this laboratory."

"It's yours, and the freedom of the rest of the house."

"There is an atmosphere of peace here."

"You'll like my wife."

Billig took a roll of bills from his wallet. "May I ask you to return this to Mr. Howard Crenshaw? I can take care of that patient of mine now—in St. Damian's hospital."

Gamadge stripped off two hundred-dollar bills. "For Heaven's sake, Doctor! You took care of Barton Crenshaw for three weeks."

Billig accepted the bills. "Perhaps I am entitled to these."

"I'll send the rest to Crenshaw's lawyer—from an anonymous sympathizer. Crenshaw probably has many such by this time; they always do."

When the doctor had gone Gamadge returned to the library; a cool, pleasant August evening; one of the first of the cool nights. But after the fifteenth of August it was often cool in New York.

The doorbell rang. He would have refused himself to guests, but when he saw old Theodore's face in the door way he asked instead: "What's the matter? Who is it?"

"Mist' Gamadge."

"Well?"

"Lady calling."

"What lady?"

Theodore dumbly extended a card on a tray.

CHAPTER TWENTY-ONE

Colophon

THE LIGHT HAD NOT BEEN turned on in the office. Gamadge went in and put his hand out to a switch, but his visitor said: "Please don't. I asked your butler not to."

"Won't you sit down, Mrs. Crenshaw?"

"I'm only staying a minute."

She stood beside the desk, dressed as she had been at their last meeting, except for the little mourning veil. No words passed between them until she said: "I ought to have let him have the divorce. Will it help him if I say so?"

"His lawyer will know, Mrs. Crenshaw."

"We haven't talked it over yet—what I'm to say. I ought to have listened when he asked me to let him have the divorce. But it was such a shock—and I thought it was a whim; I thought he'd get over it. We didn't quarrel; not even about that. He knew I always meant what I said. I never once thought of Lucette."

"You mustn't think that it was only Lucette Daker."

"Wasn't it?" She seemed faintly surprised, but without mental energy to protest.

"He wanted another life—while there was time. It was a frenzy."

"I hope they'll say so at the trial. He can't be himself even now. Of course he won't see *me*—I didn't expect him to. He won't talk to anybody. I got him that lawyer."

"You got the best there is."

"He says I could go into a sanitarium and not be a witness at all. He said they'd never make me."

"They won't."

"But of course I'll be a witness; to say it was all because I wouldn't let him have the divorce. Why did I keep thinking that because he once loved me he would again?"

"Everybody thinks that; they can't help it."

"Well." She had been looking out into the dusk; now she turned to him. "I mustn't take up your time; I thought I'd just stop in and get that book."

"The Shakespeare?"

"If he ever wants his things again he might as well have them."

"Of course."

Gamadge went to the filing cabinet and got out the Shakespeare. He laid it open on the desk, and rubbed out what pencil marks remained—those between the lines. She seemed incurious; but she said: "It *is* dreadfully battered, isn't it?"

"I'll wrap it up for you."

While he got paper and string she went on: "Barton Crenshaw must have come that evening while I was spending the night in San Francisco. Howard never read much; I was always at him to read the books from the Club, and I was always at him not to spend money. I wonder what it *was* that disgusted him so."

Gamadge wrapped the book and handed it to her. When she had taken it from him she stood looking at him gravely. "I'll remember what you said," she told him. "About Howard being driven. I must say the right things."

"You'll do whatever can be done, Mrs. Crenshaw. There's no doubt of that."

"Goodnight; and thanks very much."

Theodore was in the hall, waiting respectfully to usher this tragic visitor out into the twilight. When the front door had closed behind her Gamadge went upstairs and telephoned to Schenck.

"Hello." Schenck sounded jubilant. "What's new?"

"Evidence. Crenshaw is done for, and Billig is out."

"We must celebrate."

"I'm not quite in the mood. Mrs. Crenshaw was here."

"No!"

"To get the Shakespeare. I owe her an apology—she doesn't want Lucette Daker boiled in oil; she isn't thinking of her at all."

"What is she thinking about?"

"About how to convince a judge and a jury that it was all her fault; that she sent Crenshaw out of his head temporarily, you know—and that she's entirely to blame."

"Naturally she doesn't want him electrocuted; what would they say in Sundown, California?"

"It isn't entirely that. She's not a great soul, oh no; she's still the woman who wouldn't go to Crenshaw's funeral; but then she thought her husband had been actuated towards her by petty spite. Now she understands that it was a bigger thing than that; he really wasn't thinking of her at all, he was only trying to get out. Get out. But how many women in her place would take the blame? I thought she'd turn into a fury and ruin any chance Crenshaw might have."

"It's shock; she's crushed for the time being—she'll get over it."

"No, she won't."

"Look here; you need diversion. I'm giving a cocktail party for Irene."

"Who?"

"Irene Pender."

"That's the boy."

"Do you think Clara would come up for it?"

"If it's a serious occasion, of course she will."

Schenck cleared his throat. "It's serious."

"Good for you both."

"She's too good for me, Gamadge; nice old family, old house, heirlooms; and some money from her grandmother."

"And an excellent disposition."

"We ought to have a pretty good time together. She just suits me, Gamadge."

"I bet she never has another nervous breakdown as long as she lives."

"Nervous breakdown? What do you mean? She's absolutely the most balanced person I ever met—in every way. What gave you the idea that she had nervous breakdowns?"

"I don't know."